Drake has just met the woman of his dreams, but his mother has other ideas.

Picking up his mother's letter, he pulled from the white parchment envelope a single sheet of paper that had words carefully printed on it, and not a single comment from Katherine Forrest:

> *luscious hair*
> *peaches-and-cream complexion*
> *late twenties*
> *smart and beautiful*

Curious and puzzled, Drake turned the paper over. There was nothing written on the back to tell him who this intriguing female was. His natural inclination was to scrunch the paper into a ball and toss it in the trash as meaningless, except that his mother never sent him something meaningless.

He read the description again, then growled deep in his throat as awareness dawned on him. Snaring the portable phone from the hutch behind him, he called her.

"I know what you're doing," he said when a lyrical soprano voice answered the ring.

"And what is that, dear?" Katherine Forrest responded.

"You're matchmaking."

"You're absolutely right."

"You admit it, without shame?"

"Freely. I have found the perfect wife for you."

KATHLEEN YAPP lives in Georgia with her husband, Ken; they have four children and six grand-children. She is an accomplished writer of both con-temporary and historical romances.

Books by Kathleen Yapp

HEARTSONG PRESENTS

HP70—A New Song

Don't miss out on any of our super romances. Write to us at the following address for information on our newest releases and club information.

Heartsong Presents Readers' Service
P.O. Box 719
Uhrichsville, OH 44683

A Match
Made in Heaven

Kathleen Yapp

Heartsong Presents

A note from the Author:

DEDICATION

With love, and smiles, to David and Tamara.   You know why.

SPECIAL THANKS

To Tamara McCumber, for her patient explanation of the technical aspects of the data communications industry.

I love to hear from my readers! You may write to me at the following address:

> **Kathleen Yapp**
> **Author Relations**
> **P.O. Box 719**
> **Uhrichsville, OH 44683**

ISBN 1-55748-584-4

A MATCH MADE IN HEAVEN

PRINTED IN THE U.S.A.

prologue

"Your son would be a perfect husband for my daughter," Jane Grady announced to Katherine Forrest as they ate lunch together in a small, elegant restaurant in northeast Georgia.

"And your daughter would be a perfect wife for my son," Katherine agreed, looking at a picture of a stunning, red-haired young woman whose eyes sparkled with life. "What are we going to do about it?"

"Get them together, of course."

"How?"

"First, we'll pique their curiosity." Jane Grady smiled and sipped her sweetened iced tea.

"Every few days tell them something intriguing about each other." Katherine Forrest smiled and sipped her lemon-flavored water.

"Exactly."

"What fun!"

"It will be a match made in heaven," the two matrons agreed as they bowed their heads, closed their eyes, and asked the Lord's guidance in their meddling.

one

C.G. Grady had one of those infectious smiles that made folks want to smile back. It started in her magnanimous heart, beamed through alert, Wedgwood blue eyes, and came out on soft, full lips over dew-white teeth that were near-perfect, except for one incisor, on the right, which barely overlapped its neighbor.

Women wanted to be her friend; men did, too. It was a rare day when C.G. Grady was not smiling about something.

Today was a rare day. Not only was she not smiling, she was frowning, for she had just been told that Ashford Bank and Trust, for which she worked as Manager of the Information Systems Division, was being acquired by a major bank in Atlanta.

"All twelve of our branches here in northeast Georgia will become part of Georgia National Bank the middle of December," one of the vice presidents told her. "We are assured that most of our people will retain their present positions." He cleared his throat. "Most, but not all. Your performance during this acquisition could be a contributing factor in whether you stay or go."

The fifty-three-year-old vice president leaned forward over his uncluttered mahogany desk. "I certainly hope you will be one of those who will stay, C.G. How could we get along without your 'joie de vivre'?"

C.G. was more concerned about how she would get on without a paycheck, and wished she had more money in her savings account. She'd paid too much for the used car she'd just bought, and maybe she should cancel that New Year's cruise to the Bahamas she'd bought as a surprise for her parents.

"Do you know with whom I'll be working on merging the data information of the two banks?" she asked the vice president.

"Yes, his name is Drake Forrest. I just got a memo on him this morning. He's an independent communications consultant with an outstanding reputation."

Drake Forrest? She'd read about him not more than a month ago, in *Fortune* magazine. The article had said he was one of the best consultants in the country, constantly in demand by Fortune 500 Service Companies.

"I wonder what he's like to work with?" she thought out loud.

"Tough, I hear through the grapevine. Thorough, cost conscious. Nothing stands in the way of his completing a job on schedule."

"Nothing? What about tornadoes, civil war, the discovery of gold in the parking lot?"

"Nothing," the vice president affirmed, and C.G. groaned while he smiled at her sense of humor.

She didn't mind hard work and long hours, but Drake Forrest sounded like a tyrant, albeit an exciting tyrant of such knowledge and reputation from whom she could learn a lot, if all went well.

Of course, if all did not go well, she could lose her job.

Returning to her own office, a carpeted, nice-sized room behind glass windows on the left side of the bank's luxurious lobby, she thought of the seven years she'd worked there. They'd been good years, and she'd learned and been promoted, until now her department, comprised of herself and two assistants, had responsibility for all data regarding account records, credit histories, and loan information for twelve separate Ashford Bank and Trust facilities.

She was good at her job and had been told so by her superiors many more times than once. But would the executives of Georgia National think so, too? Would Drake Forrest think so?

C.G. sat down in her chair behind her desk and reached for the blue leather New King James Bible on its left corner. Her fingers easily flew to Isaiah 26:3, the verse she'd read that very morning as part of her devotions: "You will keep him in perfect peace, whose mind is stayed on You, because he trusts in You."

I do trust You, Lord, she prayed silently, her eyes open and staring ahead at nothing in particular, *with all my heart and soul and mind. Help me in these trying days ahead. Don't let me goof up. I'm not a rich girl, and I need this job. I pray in Jesus' name.*

Knowing she'd better be prepared for the inevitable first contact, C.G. called her assistants, James Wyatt, who handled data operations, and Dottie Westfall, whose responsibilities were voice communications, into her office to tell them about the acquisition.

They were stunned.

"Are we going to be fired?" James asked. He was a short, wiry young man of thirty-one, two years older than C.G., and though hard-working and intelligent, he was not innovative or easy to get to know. C.G. expected he would never rise far in the corporate world.

"I certainly hope not," she answered his anxious question.

"New companies like to bring in their own people, C.G., or tighten up and let employees go."

"That's true."

"Don't worry about it, James," C.G.'s other assistant, Dottie Westfall, told him with a wave of the hand. She was a hefty woman with orange-blonde hair, ten years older than C.G., and married to a career policeman with whom she had four children.

Dottie was brutally honest, all the time, and perfectly content to be an assistant and nothing more. "I have enough responsibility at home," she had said to C.G. more than once, "taking care of four kids because Hank seems always to be on duty. If he put in as much time with his family as he does at the station, we'd have a good life."

"Just like you-know-who," C.G., had quipped, thinking of the breakup of her engagement three years before to an attorney who was also a workaholic. Randolph was forever striving to impress the senior partners at his prestigious law firm with how many hours he billed clients. The only time he had lavished attention on C.G. had been when he was trying to win her affections. Once the conquest was complete, and an impressive diamond shone on her third finger, left hand, he went back to his real love: practicing law.

The engagement had lasted five months before C.G. had broken it off. By that time there had been no tears to shed, but she had learned an indelible lesson: beware of men married to their careers, they can only handle one wife at a time. This thought brought her back to the present.

"We'll be working with a hotshot, independent consultant, a Drake Forrest," C.G. told her assistants, "who gets the job done regardless of how many bodies get strewed along the way."

James groaned, but Dottie laughed. "I can hardly wait to meet him," she said. She grabbed James by the shoulders and pushed him toward the door of C.G.'s office. "Come on, partner, we'd better sharpen our pencils and straighten up our desks before Hotshot gets here."

"My desk is always neat," James protested, as Dottie propelled him out the door.

C.G. smiled. They were good people, James and Dottie. *I hope their jobs won't be in jeopardy,* she thought, knowing it was her responsibility not only to make a good impression of herself, but of her co-workers as well.

For the next two hours, she closed the door to her office, kicked off her shoes under her desk, and went over the information she was sure Drake Forrest would need. There was a lot. It would not be a quick and easy task to merge the information systems of the two banks. It was now the first week in August. To complete everything by mid-December was going to take some doing, but she would be ready.

She wondered when he would contact her.

&

It was only a nagging pain in her shoulders and neck that reminded C.G. she'd been sitting in one position for too long.

Standing, and stretching, which felt deliciously good, she looked to the left, through the glass wall into the expansive lobby of the bank, and her eyes collided with those of a tall, strikingly handsome, blond man standing in the center of the room, who was staring in her direction.

She stared back, for though he wore a finely-tailored business suit and carried an expensive-looking briefcase, he seemed—as he stood there, square on both legs, his expression fiercely serious—more like a conquering Viking warrior, transported out of history to capture this very room. And her.

Her eyes left his full head of windblown, sandy-colored hair and traveled over well-developed shoulders and chest, past slim hips, long legs, down to his wing-tipped shoes, and back up to his rugged face marked by large eyes and a prominent, slightly off-center nose. His fierce look had been replaced by a rakish grin, and C.G. was humiliated that he'd caught her ogling.

Since no one else was paying him any attention, she quickly left her office and hurried toward him, knowing, just knowing he was Drake Forrest, already here and ready to put her on a work treadmill she wouldn't get off for months.

A phone call of warning would have been nice, she thought snappishly, as she stopped in front of him, a tiny bit breathless, and looked up, and up, into the most compelling, blue eyes she had ever seen. Her heart stopped.

Drake Forrest watched the woman walk toward him with a self-assured gait, and he liked what he saw. She was stunning and not too tall, with smooth, red hair swirled casually about her chin, pale, luminescent skin, and huge, vibrant eyes that held his attention.

Her stylish cream-colored suit, hemmed just below the knee, and fastened at the waist with one, large, cloth-covered button, covered a slender body and identified the wearer as a woman of taste.

She belongs here, in this sophisticated room, he thought, *surrounded by refinement and important business.*

The impressive, mahogany desks, gold-framed nature pictures on the walls, healthy green floor plants, thick, sound-absorbing, slate blue carpeting, tellers speaking in subdued voices, and even the seven-foot grandfather clock standing imperiously in one corner—all gave the impression that Ashford Bank and Trust was a proper place, a bank to be trusted to handle one's money wisely.

She was in front of him now, and Drake saw that her eyes were blue, her mouth small, and that her head came just about to his shoulders.

She smelled of Chanel No. 5, and the first crazy thought that entered his mind was that his mother would approve of her.

He also knew she would have a serious, romantic name like Elizabeth or Catherine. Not C.G. What kind of a name was that?

When he'd first been given the name of the person he'd be working with at Ashford Bank and Trust, he'd conjured up an image of a woman in combat boots, no makeup, and a mannish haircut. Not at all someone like the princess who stood before him now, all radiant and sweet smelling.

"Mr. Forrest?" she asked, in a voice that was pure velvet, as he had known it would be. She smiled, and her teeth, surrounded by well-shaped lips the color of Georgia Belle peaches (he loved Georgia Belle peaches), were white and straight, except for one and it wasn't a detraction.

"Yes, I'm Drake Forrest, here to see C.G. Grady," he said, wishing he could delay his meeting with "that woman" and spend time, instead, with this exquisite beauty.

"I'm C.G. Grady," she said, giving him a smile that could stop a train on its tracks.

Shocked, and without taking his eyes from her heart-shaped face, because he never wanted to, Drake extended his hand to her, which she accepted and shook with delicate firmness. Only the strongest self-control kept him from raising her fingers to his lips.

"I look forward to working with you, Mr. Forrest," she said, her intelligent eyes assuring him she was capable of doing that well. "My assistants and I will do all that we can to help you."

"Good."

"If you'll follow me to my office, then," she said, gesturing toward it, "we'll get started."

Drake silently obeyed. Never a follower, always a leader, at the moment he was quite content to do as he was bidden.

In her office, he sat down in the low-backed chair in front of her desk, and watched her settle herself, smoothing her skirt beneath her in the time-old tradition of women who cared about the appearance of their clothes.

He thought of what he'd been told about her at GNB: "C.G. Grady is whip-smart and dependable. That's all we know. It'll be your decision whether we keep her or bring in someone else."

He couldn't tell yet whether she could keep up with his demands, but he would cut her no slack. Gorgeous and sweet-smelling though she was, either she did the job, or she was out the door.

two

"Mr. Forrest, what do you need from my division?" C.G. asked, noticing the strong set of his jaw, the straight, well-shaped nose, the way his eyes focused on her.

"The specifications for your computer system and its software, and a month's billing for voice and data communications."

"Of course. Shall I bring the information to you at GNB's headquarters in Atlanta?"

"No, just send it by overnight mail to my company." He handed her a business card, which she accepted, noting he worked in a prestigious area of north Atlanta. "If everything goes smoothly, Miss Grady, you'll find I'm an easy man to work with."

His strong, straight mouth edged up at the corners, but C.G. wasn't fooled. She knew there was more to that sentence, and she finished it silently: *And if it doesn't go smoothly, you're out of a job.*

"Georgia National wants this acquisition completed by December 15," he told her in a rich, deep voice that would do justice to Shakespeare, "and I don't want our part in it to cause any holdups."

"Nor do I, Mr. Forrest."

"Then I can expect the information I need tomorrow?"

"Yes, you may."

C.G. liked Drake Forrest's professionalism. He was direct and didn't waste time. There'd be no idle chitchat from him asking about her weekend or how her rose garden was doing. His no-nonsense approach was, "Here's the schedule; stick to it. And survive."

His presence filled her office with a potent masculinity, fostered by his self-confidence and strong, decisive body language—the way he moved, and stood, and took possession of the space in which he found himself.

Probably a little older than she, his rugged good looks and mesmerizing eyes started her nerves tingling whenever he spoke to her, and C.G. knew it would take some doing to concentrate on their work and not on him.

"I'm having an office prepared for you now," she said, wondering if he ever relaxed, cracked a joke, was late in the morning. "Is there anything in particular you need in it?"

"Just an IBM-compatible computer, mouse, printer, fax, phone, yellow tablets for my scribbling, #2 pencils, felt-tipped pens in an assortment of colors, and any other general office supplies you can think of."

"No coffee?"

"Yes, definitely coffee. Thanks. I drink it black."

"Lunch menus from nearby restaurants? Pizza coupons?"

The corners of his mouth twitched and he gave her a questioning gaze. "Whatever you think I'll need, Miss Grady."

"Please call me C.G."

"Which stands for?"

"C.G."

"Ah," he said, his eyes dancing with a mischief she was surprised to see. "A secret name?"

"Known only to my parents, minister, and doctor."

"Not to a husband?"

"No."

"Boyfriend?"

C.G. stood up without answering the question. "Drake—I assume I may call you that—name, rank, and serial number is all I can give you today." The rebuke was a gentle one and she waited for his reaction. Her personal life was her personal life, and none of his business.

When his handsome, chiseled face relaxed in what could almost be called a smile, almost, she added, "I think we'll work well together."

Then the smile became thoughtful, almost enigmatic, and oozed over C.G. with all the devastation of hot fudge melting over ice cream. "I hope you'll say that four months from now, C.G. I have been known to eat alive those who don't live up to what's expected."

She laughed. "Then you won't find a meal here."

"Good."

Were his eyes twinkling? Under that stern personality, did there lurk a sense of humor? C.G. determined to find out, not entirely frightened by his gruff manner, but wisely respectful of him, as one would respect the territory of a predatory animal.

Her main goal was to hold her own against him, and help James and Dottie to do the same.

Another goal, which might prove harder to realize, if he was not married, and if he kept looking at her the way he had been so far, would be to keep herself from being drawn into a personal relationship with him, because she had a hard and fast rule NEVER to mix her business and personal life. NEVER.

"I'll start using that office next week," Drake told her, standing up.

"It will be ready."

He picked up his briefcase, laid it on her desk, opened it up, and handed her two sheets of paper neatly typed.

"I've made some notes about the areas we should cover first."

C.G. scanned them and saw nothing that would present a problem. She told him so.

"In that case, it's been a pleasure, C.G., to meet you." He gave her a broad smile that weakened her knees.

"Thank you, Drake."

After he left, her office felt unbelievably empty, and C.G. placed her hands on her cheeks, knowing they were warm, as a quick glance in the decorative, beveled glass mirror above her credenza verified.

Taking a moment to calm her accelerated pulse, she finally buzzed both her assistants and asked them to come to her office.

"I have a major assignment that needs to be completed yesterday," she told them.

Like it or not, they were up and running with Drake Forrest, and if they wanted to keep their jobs, they dared not miss a step.

❧

Drake left C.G. Grady's office and took the first ordinary breath he'd had in ten minutes. That's all it had taken for the woman to impress the life out of him and speed up his heart rate. He knew it was not going to be easy working closely with her without getting personally involved, which was not a good idea in a work situation, usually.

With C.G. Grady, he was sure it was going to be downright impossible, for she was intelligent as well as beautiful, organized as well as intriguing, businesslike as well as womanlike. And, she wasn't afraid of him, which would make their getting to know each other a whole lot easier.

He laughed at himself for thinking, with a name of C.G., that she would be mannish and wear combat boots. *What could those initials stand for?* he wondered. Right now, to him, they stood for confident and gorgeous.

❧

The rest of Drake's day was filled with finishing up work for other companies so he could devote full attention to the GNB acquisition. The rest of his day was also filled with thoughts of C.G. Grady.

At his apartment that night, he was still thinking about her as he paced back and forth in his kitchen, restlessly watching a thick steak grilling on the Jenn-Air cooktop. He remembered the sheen of her hair and the charming, musical lilt of her voice that made him want to hang on every word.

The juices from the T-bone sizzled on its top and made him think she was feisty under her office decorum, and as he flipped the steak over with long-handled tongs, he wondered why there was not a man in her life. That had been the first thing he had looked for when he'd entered her office and she'd turned around to face him: a ring. There hadn't been one.

The beeper on the microwave signalled his baked potato was done, so Drake whipped it out, slit open the top with a Ginzu knife, and dropped in a hunk of butter the size of a golf ball.

When the steak was cooked, he added it to the plate with the potato, generously sprinkled them both with salt, and took from the freezer an icy glass mug in which he poured cold, whole milk. Taking a long, slow drink, he sank into a chair at his white oak kitchen table and began his meal.

Drake was a good cook, although his menus were few and basic. He was not into salads or quiche or casseroles. Meat and potatoes were his staple, along with fresh vegetables, an apple a day, and pecans. He loved Georgia pecans.

Savoring the odor of the medium-rare steak, he cut off one piece and plunged it into his mouth. "Mmmm," he groaned in satisfaction, and worked the melted butter through the baked potato, before stabbing a forkful of that into his mouth.

Relaxing for the first time since he'd hit the front door of his large apartment in trendy, uptown Buckhead in north Atlanta, he looked contentedly around the cheerful breakfast nook with its white chair molding and white and burgundy wallpaper where green ivy leaves trailed. Through wide windows, their white shutters open, early evening light streamed.

Drake liked light and space, each room in the apartment having only minimal furnishings that were, however, big, comfortable, and always expensive.

He was outrageously successful at what he did, with the bank account and man-toys to prove it, but he worked hard and expected others around him to do the same. That would include C.G. Grady.

The classic beauty of her face surged back into his memory, and Drake knew he was in trouble. He couldn't stop thinking about her.

He rarely was without a date on the weekend. His little black book was filled with names and addresses of the women he'd taken out. Some had stayed in his life for a month or two; most lasted only a few weeks.

Their common appeal was good looks and intelligence. They were all career women who knew how to dress and speak and present themselves well. They had captured his interest quickly, and just as quickly had lost it. They were nice, but not impossible to live without.

Would C.G. Grady be different?

Time will tell, he decided, slicing more of his steak into bite-sized pieces, *that is, if she ever lets me get close to her.* And he knew, even in this short time of acquaintance, that he definitely wanted to get close to her.

three

To stop thinking of C.G., Drake concentrated on devouring his meal, quicker than he'd been taught to as a boy, and as he did, he remembered a letter he'd received from his mother that day.

She and his father only lived fifty miles away, in a small town of twenty-one thousand in north Georgia, but she loved to write letters and send him tidbits of information she'd gleaned from newspapers and magazines that she thought would interest him. It was like having his own private clipping service, for his mother was an intelligent woman who understood pretty well the complicated world of communications through which he moved.

He respected his parents, and they got along well even though they, actually his mother, did remind him now and then that he worked too hard (in her opinion but not his) and should be getting married and having children.

At 35, he guessed she was right, at least about the marriage and family, but he'd never met the woman who could make him forget his passion—business—for more than a few hours.

Picking up his mother's letter, he pulled from the white parchment envelope a single sheet of paper that had words carefully printed on it, and not a single comment from Katherine Forrest:

luscious hair
peaches-and-cream complexion
late twenties
smart and beautiful

Curious and puzzled, Drake turned the paper over. There was nothing written on the back to tell him who this intriguing female was. His natural inclination was to scrunch the paper into a ball and toss it in the trash as meaningless, except that his

18

mother never sent him something meaningless.

He read the description again, then growled deep in his throat as awareness dawned on him. Snaring the portable phone from the hutch behind him, he called her.

"I know what you're doing," he said when a lyrical soprano voice answered the ring.

"And what is that, dear?" Katherine Forrest responded.

"You're matchmaking."

"You're absolutely right."

"You admit it, without shame?"

"Freely. I have found the perfect wife for you."

Drake chuckled. "Mother, I'm a big boy. I hang up my clothes, pick out my own socks, and even know how to open a can of spaghetti. And, someday, I'll find my own wife."

"A good wife."

"Sure."

"A Christian wife."

He paused. "I suppose so."

He knew his mother was not at all sure he would find a Christian wife, and to be honest, it wasn't the first requirement to being attracted to a woman, though he certainly wasn't opposed to the idea.

An uncomfortable silence reminded Drake that his parents were concerned that over the years he had slipped away from the close relationship he had once had with God when he'd been a teenager.

It wasn't that he disbelieved, far from it. His priorities had just changed as he'd matured. He knew this attitude hurt his folks, and for that he was sorry, but a man had to live his own life, and he still considered himself a Christian, albeit an inactive one.

"You haven't set up a time for me to meet this incomparable person, have you?" Drake asked, dreading the answer if it were yes.

"No, son, not yet, but I'm working on it." The lilt was there in her voice. She had forced herself past the awkward moment.

"Please don't."

"You'll like her, I know. You have so much in common."

Drake was not going to fall into the trap of asking what they had in common. He wasn't going to cooperate at all.

"Mother, give it up."

"I can't. She's right for you. I know it. Her mother knows it."

"Her mother?"

"Yes, we go to different churches but attend a community Bible study and have become friends."

Drake groaned and stared up at the ceiling. The only thing worse for a man than having a matchmaking mother was having two mothers trying to manipulate him into matrimony.

"I love you, Mother, you know that, but please do not set me up with this stranger. Does she know what you and her mother are doing?"

"No, she doesn't. But she will."

"Mother—"

"Good-bye, dear."

The line went dead and Drake's jaw turned to steel.

&

C.G. Grady kicked off her leather low heels and collapsed onto the blueberry camelback sofa in her living room whose ambience was defined by comfortable furniture, well-cared-for plants, stained glass suncatchers hanging in the front windows, and brass-framed pictures of family and friends.

Hers was a country house, and she'd purposely decorated it to have a close, cozy atmosphere.

It had been a disturbing day at the bank, and never had she been more thankful for the quiet and solitude of her charming, eight-year-old house.

Propping her feet up on the heavy oak coffee table in front of her, she closed her eyes, loving to be here, where the antique clock ticked comfortingly on the mantel over the gas log fireplace, the air conditioning hummed, keeping the temperature in the one-story, seven-room home a steady seventy-eight degrees, and the crockpot on the kitchen counter gave out the tantalizing odor of a tuna-noodle casserole, her favorite. She loved casseroles.

C.G. breathed deeply and slowly, deciding that after a few more minutes of immobility, she would take a leisurely, warm bath with plenty of scented bubbles to soak away the day's stresses. Maybe then, she would stop thinking of Drake Forrest, and how he'd looked, in the lobby of the bank, when he'd burst into her life at three forty-five that afternoon.

He was an interesting man and typical of the breed who put work above all else. Of course, she didn't know that about him for sure, but she'd be surprised if she were wrong. It was all there: the decisiveness, the single-mindedness, the fire in the eyes when discussing an important project.

Oh, yes, she'd seen it all before. In her uncle, in Dottie's husband, and in the man she'd been going to marry but discovered, before it was too late, that he would always put work before her.

And now here was another one, a driven-to-succeed man who would be her superior for months to come, a man who would hold the fate of her employment in his hand and would not understand if she wanted a life outside the bank.

Picking up the mail she'd dumped on the cushion beside her when she'd first come in, she found three bills and an elegant, ivory envelope with her name and address hand-printed in the lovely, distinguishable style of her mom.

C.G. opened the envelope, anticipating some tidbit of information gleaned from a newspaper or magazine and sent on for her perusal. Jane Grady often did this even though she and C.G.'s father lived less than a mile away. C.G. smiled as she pulled out a single slip of paper.

"What is it this time, Mom?" she said out loud. "A recipe? The dates of a play you want us to see together? A new fact from history you know I'll question and. . . ."

Her voice dropped off as she read the few words carefully printed on the page:

> *wavy, blond hair*
> *mischievous eyes*
> *strong*
> *dependable*

Curious, and puzzled, C.G. frowned and turned the paper over. There was nothing on the back. She reread the few statistics. "WHO has wavy, blond hair and mischievous eyes?" she asked the empty room.

Sighing, and not at all in the mood for a game, she decided to take her bath and then call her mom and find out what she was up to.

An hour later, refreshed and ravenous for dinner, she forgot to do so.

❧

The phone call came in at 11:58 a.m. the next day at the bank, just as C.G. was starting to think about lunch. She recognized the deep, resonant voice.

"Drake, good morning. How are you today?"

"Twiddling my thumbs, Miss Grady."

"I beg your pardon?"

"I didn't receive the information you promised me."

C.G.'s mouth dropped open. "It went out yesterday. Overnight, express mail."

"Yes, I received a packet from your office, but it wasn't what I wanted."

"What's missing?"

"Figures from all twelve of your branches. All I got were the ones for the main office where you work."

C.G. groaned. She had specifically told James and Dottie to include every branch of Ashford Bank and Trust. Why hadn't they?

"I'm sorry for the mistake, Drake."

"Did you personally handle this, C.G.?"

"No, I didn't."

"Why?"

The question was curt and C.G. wanted to snap back that she

did have other work to do, but she held her tongue, not about to
shift the blame from herself to her assistants. She was in charge.
The responsibility was hers.

"Let me look into the matter and call you back," she offered.

"Forget the call. I'll be there in an hour to pick it up."

"But, Drake—"

A rude click told C.G. the conversation was ended, and she
decided right then and there not to serve him tea and crumpets
when he appeared.

four

C.G. called James and Dottie to her office. "We have a problem," she announced.

James's shoulders drooped. "What is it?"

"We were supposed to send figures from all twelve of our branches to Drake Forrest. Instead, he only received ones from our main office here."

Dottie grunted and poked James' arm. "I told you that's what he wanted."

"I'm sorry, C.G. We goofed. I goofed," James apologized, his gaze falling to the floor.

C.G. felt sorry for him, knowing he was a real team player, always willing to do whatever needed doing, whatever would please her.

When he'd first come to the bank three years before, he had asked to date her socially, but she'd let him know she never mixed her business and personal life. Besides, she was not at all attracted to him.

She came to learn that even though James treated women with great courtesy, he was not a lady's man, and was sensitive about his slight build and five-foot eight-inch height, as though that were why women didn't like him. Actually, she thought him nice looking, with straight, brown hair and pale, sensitive eyes, and hoped he would find someone to love.

Dottie was a contrast to him, being twenty pounds overweight, with short, kinky hair, fat cheeks, and a cheerful, never-get-discouraged disposition that sometimes drove James crazy. C.G. had always been able to count on Dottie. Until now.

"I'm sorry, too," Dottie added her apology to James'. "We'll gather the rest of the information and get it out stat."

C.G. forced a smile. "Yes, on getting the material together. No, on sending it out. As we speak, a disgruntled Drake Forrest is on his way here to pick it up."

James turned and ran out of the office.

❧

Thirty minutes later Dottie hurried into C.G.'s office and leaned over, palms down, on C.G.'s mahogany desk. Her cheeks were flushed. "I have the scoop on Drake Forrest," she said excitedly.

C.G. looked up from a file she'd been rifling through. "I don't need 'the scoop,' Dottie; I need the information he wants."

"James is finishing up. This is better. My cousin, Mattie, works for Georgia National in Atlanta, and is dating a man who's worked with Drake Forrest on another project, and she says that he says—"

"Hold it, Dottie." C.G. put up both hands. "Is this gossip?"

Twinkly eyes accompanied a twinkly grin. "Of course not. It's ammunition, for you, as well as us. We're all fighting for our jobs here, C.G."

"I agree. Go ahead."

Dottie spoke softly and quickly.

"Drake Forrest. Thirty-five. Unmarried. No children. Born in Chicago. Grew up in Southern California. Graduated from Cal State Fullerton. Seven years with Citibank, at the end of which, get this, he was in charge of communications for the *entire nation*. Then he quit, went on his own, and in only five years has built a solid reputation as the best in his field."

"That's impressive."

"You said it. He's successful, rich, good-looking, and dates a different woman every month."

C.G. stood up. "We don't need to know about his women."

"Forewarned is forearmed."

"He's not pursuing us, Dottie."

Dottie shrugged. "Us? No. You? Time will tell."

❧

Exactly fifty-two minutes later, Drake Forrest strode into C.G.'s office and plunked his Italian leather briefcase down on her desk.

Startled, and surprised that he'd made it there so fast, C.G. looked up past a custom-tailored charcoal suit, gray shirt, silver tie bar, and a silver, burgundy, and black silk tie, her eyes finally colliding with his stormy blue ones. "You broke the speed limit, Mr. Forrest," she said sweetly.

"Did I?" His jaw flexed. "Don't you ever drive faster than you should, C.G.?"

"Never."

"Never?"

"Well, hardly ever."

He gave her a superior look, then asked, "Do you have the information I need?"

"That, and more I know you'll be wanting." From the way his eyes never left hers, C.G. felt a strange heat playing at the back of her neck as she handed him a heavy folder.

C.G.'s smile softened Drake's heart as he took the folder from her. He liked the fact that she was mentally quick, could spar with words, and wasn't going to let him intimidate her, not that he'd planned to. It was just his nature to take charge of every situation.

His eyes skimmed over the data. It was exactly what he'd come for, and he was impressed that C.G. had gathered additional information for him before he'd asked for it. Now he could get back to his office and bury himself in it all, but he hesitated, not wanting to leave, and knowing why: he wanted to be with her.

"I think I'd better look these over now," he said, "to be sure everything's here."

"Of course," C.G. agreed. "Let me show you the office I've arranged for you to use while you're here, and introduce you to Greta, my secretary, who will help whenever you need her."

"Fine."

She stood, and the rustle of her sage green silk dress pleased his ears as did the scent of her perfume when she passed him. Again, she was wearing Chanel. Again, his nostrils deeply breathed it in and evoked an image of warm, humid nights in the arms of a beautiful woman. C.G. Grady.

He followed her through the lobby and down a short corridor to a small office, furnished stylishly, but with no windows.

Reading his mind she said, "I'm sorry we don't have a room with a view."

"No problem," he assured her. And it wasn't. "When I'm working, I'm not gazing out a window to look at daisies."

"Then the room is adequate?"

"Let's see."

He moved to the desk, opened its drawers, saw the well-stocked supplies he had requested, sat down in the high backed executive chair, played with the computer, asked C.G. a few questions about the phone system, examined the printer and fax machine, then thudded the palms of both hands down on the desk as he stood up.

"It'll do fine." He was rewarded by a luscious smile that made him aware of how soft and inviting her lips were.

"I'll leave you to your work, then," she said, and was almost out the door before Drake called after her, "You will be in your office, won't you, in case I have any questions?"

She looked down at a slim, gold watch at her wrist. "I was about to go to lunch. . ."

Drake glanced at his Rolex. "It is that time, isn't it? Why don't we go together?"

"I. . .uh. . ." C.G. stammered, and Drake almost galloped across the room to get to her.

"Are you going with someone else?"

"Well. . .no."

"Have errands to run?"

"No."

"Good." He took her elbow and escorted her back toward the lobby, their footsteps muffled by the thick, durable carpet. "Just guide me to a good restaurant. I'll drive." He grinned down at her. "Slowly."

After she'd picked up her purse in her office, Drake escorted C.G. to his black Corvette convertible, top up since rain was expected. He opened the passenger door for her, and watched her get in, hoping he could keep his head when she was sitting close to him, her perfume filling his car, her dress shimmering in the sunlight streaming through the window, catching its hues.

Following the directions C.G. gave him, and driving slowly (something he rarely did) through the downtown streets of Cheston, Drake saw that it was an ordinary, small town, nothing spectacular or memorable about it, except for the abundant pines, Bradford pear trees, crepe myrtles, and beds of saucy petunias, marigolds, and impatiens which brightened the landscape at practically every building.

"We're here," C.G. announced. "Turn right and park."

Drake did and found himself in the parking lot of a four-story hospital. Gazing up at the neat brick building, he said, "We're eating lunch at the hospital?"

"Yes. They have great food."

"You're kidding me."

"Would I do that?"

Drake got out of the car and was halfway around when C.G. opened her door.

"Stay where you are," he shouted, hurrying to help her out. "No woman riding in my car ever opens her own door."

C.G. gave him an appreciative gaze that warmed his skin clear to his shoes. "I'm not used to such gentlemanly care, Mr. Forrest. Please forgive me."

Drake stared into her vivid, blue eyes and wondered what was wrong with the men of Cheston that they would not give C.G. Grady the care she deserved.

"The food really is wonderful here," she said as they walked up the stairs to the hospital entrance, "and we can eat fast." They waited for the elevator to take them to the lower floor where the cafeteria was located.

"I thought you didn't like fast."

"Not in cars, but in food it's good, especially when one has something to do after lunch."

"Does one have something to do after lunch?"

"Yes, there's someone I must visit, but it will only take a few minutes. We won't be late back to the office."

"I certainly hope not."

They laughed then, and Drake knew that working with C.G. was going to be nothing but pure pleasure.

five

Drake wouldn't have believed it, but he actually enjoyed his lunch. The beef pot roast was full of tender potatoes and carrots in a thick, brown gravy, the blueberry muffins were soft and warm, and the strawberry shortcake was as good as his mother made. It was hard not to go back for seconds of everything, but he settled for one more muffin. A particularly large one.

"Do you eat here often?" he asked C.G.

"Yes, because I'm here a lot, visiting members of my church who are sick."

"I see." *So*, he thought, *C.G. Grady is not only intelligent and capable, she's caring and religious, too.* Now he *knew* his mother would like her.

"The lady I'm going to see today had a mild heart attack four days ago, but she's recuperating nicely. She doesn't have much family living in the area, so a visit means a lot to her."

"And you don't mind coming to a hospital?"

She smiled. "Not at all. In fact, I get excited whenever I'm here. I think I should have been a doctor or a nurse."

Drake found himself curious to know what else she did with her free time, and he asked her.

"I love to read."

Her quick answer indicated a passion, and he liked that, always drawn to people who felt strongly about things.

"What kinds of books?"

"Almost anything: fiction, nonfiction, historical, contemporary, biographies. I really enjoy biographies. And Christian books."

Drake thought of his library and knew he had everything she liked on his shelves, except for the Christian books. He'd given them all away before he'd moved to this apartment—not enough room for everything, he'd told himself.

29

"What else?" he asked.

C.G. took a bite of lemon meringue pie and gazed thoughtfully out the window at the pretty garden area awash with scarlet red begonias around a gurgling fountain, then said enthusiastically, "I'm a big sports fan—baseball and basketball in particular."

"Really?" He was an avid Braves fan and had season tickets for the Atlanta Hawks. Maybe she'd go to a game with him if he asked.

He buttered his muffin, and C.G. watched his hands. They were strong hands, with long, solid fingers, well manicured nails. The hands of a businessman. Yet, they looked like they could build things, hammer nails, lift furniture. Was he a man of brawn as well as brain? If so, her dad would like him; he was a physical kind of guy. Always building, tinkering around the house and yard.

Drake looked up and caught her staring at him. "Am I growing tentacles?" he asked with a grin.

"Actually, I was admiring your hands."

Drake choked on the last morsel of muffin while C.G.'s cheeks flamed. "My mother says I'm too honest sometimes."

He shook his head. "I wouldn't call that a fault."

"It gets me into trouble."

"Which I'm sure you get out of with grace."

C.G. grinned. "Not always."

"I'd like to hear of a few examples."

"I'll write you a memo—some day."

Drake cleared his throat. "So, you like my hands."

C.G. looked at her watch. "Time to go if I'm to visit Mrs. Weathers and still get us back to the bank by one."

"Are you always this conscientious of company time," Drake asked, "or just trying to make an impression on me?"

C.G. gave him a serious look. "I don't play games, Drake, not with the company or in my personal life." She stood up and took her tray to a moving conveyor belt which returned it to the kitchen. Drake did the same, insisting on paying the bill, though C.G. vigorously protested.

"A quirk of mine, C.G., is always to pay when I take a lady to lunch—"

"You weren't taking me," C.G. argued. "This was a business lunch."

Drake's mouth turned up in a grin. "All right. You may pay the next time we go out."

"Fine," C.G. declared, glad she had won that battle.

It was not until she had visited her church friend, and was back in Drake's car, that she realized there would have to be another meal shared with him in order for her to pay. She wasn't sure that would be a good idea since she was beginning to like more about Drake Forrest than just his hands.

ta

The afternoon dragged by for C.G. who was acutely aware that Drake was just down the hall, going over her bank's records. She knew they were in order, that he wouldn't find anything amiss. Still, there was that nagging concern that a problem would arise.

It did.

Drake came into her office at three-thirty. He had discarded his suit jacket but his tie was still straight and the sleeves of his shirt were still buttoned at the wrist.

"I need something right away."

C.G. was sure she was going to hear that phrase a lot in the coming days: right away.

"What is it you need?"

"The total number of analog data lines for all the Ashford Bank and Trust branches, including this one. We're going to change to digital lines, which means faster transmission and fewer errors."

"I had expected that. I think there are fourteen lines altogether, but let me make sure. I'll check the phone bills for the past month and get back to you."

"Today?"

"If I can, but it could take some time to find them buried in all those numbers."

He frowned and C.G. mentally recorded two of Drake's

business priorities that she'd figured out: 1) Do it right the first time. 2) Do it as soon as you can. Simple. Like throwing the right meat to a hungry tiger. If she could manage to keep doing that with him, she just might keep her job.

"I'll wait here for you to get the figures," he said.

"Here?"

"Is there a problem with that?"

"No, except that it might take some time—"

"And you don't want me snooping around your office."

"Are you a snooper?"

Drake chuckled, despite trying not to. "Probably. A person's office tells a lot about him—or her."

C.G. gave him a saucy grin. "You could always just ask whatever it is you want to know."

"Yes, I could, but would you answer?"

"My life is an open book."

"And I enjoy reading as much as you do, C.G."

She walked hesitantly past him, not comfortable with leaving him there, in her space, 'though she wasn't sure why. The only personal things she had out were a photo of her and her parents on a sailboat, a small pewter Mickey Mouse from a favorite vacation to Disney World, and her Bible. What would he conclude from seeing those?

"C.G., are you all right?" Dottie stood up behind her small, square desk that looked as though a bomb had exploded on it. How she ever kept anything straight was beyond C.G.'s understanding. Still, her work was trustworthy.

"Yes, I'm fine," C.G. assured her with a half-hearted smile, trying to shake from her mind a picture of Drake meandering through her office. She went over to a beige, metal cabinet. "I need the phone bills file to get the exact number of analog data lines for all our branches."

"Sure, it's in there."

It was not.

Dottie looked puzzled and C.G. stared at the ceiling in frustration.

"Where is it, Dottie? Drake Forrest is waiting for those figures."

"I have no idea, C.G." Dottie rifled through the drawer herself. "Believe it or not, my files are well-organized, but that file is not where it should be."

C.G. let out an exasperated sigh. "Could James have it?"

"I don't know why. If he took it, he didn't ask me first."

They both went to his office. He wasn't there. The file C.G. needed was not on his desk and she didn't want to go rifling through his desk drawers.

Fighting a rise in temper, C.G. said, "Let's see if Greta knows anything about it."

She and Dottie went out into the lobby, to their secretary's immaculate desk at one end of the room.

"Greta," C.G. addressed the thirty-one-year-old woman, who stopped writing on a legal pad and looked up, her huge, brown eyes giving them instant attention, "we're looking for the phone bills file. Have you seen it?"

Greta pursed her lips, thinking, then absently scratched shiny brown hair that hung straight down her back and was cut in wispy bangs in the front. She shook her head no. "Not since I put last month's bill in it."

C.G. groaned and glanced back to her office, just knowing Drake Forrest was pacing a hole in the carpet and had smoke coming out of his nostrils.

Sure enough, he was not sitting patiently in the chair waiting for her return. Nor was he pacing the floor. In fact, he was not even in her office, but was, as C.G. finally located him with her eyes, in the lobby, sipping coffee and talking with one of the tellers, Susie Black, a young, tall blond with an hourglass figure and a predatory reputation where good-looking men were concerned.

six

Telling herself she didn't care how many gorgeous females Drake Forrest spoke to in the course of a day, C.G. turned back to Greta and asked, "Could James have the file we need?"

The secretary shrugged. "If he does, he got it himself. He didn't ask me to do it for him."

She and Dottie exchanged worried looks. "Thanks, Greta," C.G. said, as an uncomfortable churning began roiling up in her stomach.

She tugged on Dottie's arm and they stepped away from Greta's desk. Through clenched teeth and low voice she said, "Dottie, I *have* to find that file. I don't think I'm being melodramatic here when I say our jobs are on the line. We've already goofed once. Now we can't even find a simple file. Where is James anyway?"

"Beats me. You placate our hotshot expert, and I'll beat the bushes for James."

C.G. exhaled in frustration. "This is only the second day of the acquisition procedure. We have months of this merry-go-round ahead of us. What's next, I wonder?"

"I don't envy you, having to work with Drake Forrest. He's intense, to say the least." Then her eyes lit up. "On the other hand, he's also one gorgeous male. That physique. That thick head of hair."

"Dottie, stop drooling. You're married."

"Yes, but you're not. Maybe in a few months you'll be . . .friends with Drake Forrest."

C.G. glowered. "No, Dottie, we will not be. . .friends. You know my rule about never dating anyone from work."

"Turning down a date with James was not difficult," Dottie muttered. "Saying no to a Hungarian vegetarian dinner with 250-lb. Walter from Accounting was also not difficult. But,

34

since there isn't another eligible man in this bank, in all of
Cheston, and maybe even in the entire state of Georgia, on a par
with Drake Forrest, you may want to reconsider that ridiculous
rule."

"It is not ridiculous."

"If it makes you pass up you-know-who, it is."

"You're an impossible romantic, Dottie," C.G. insisted, and
spun around to return to her office when she ran smack into the
man of their conversation. Drake. It was like hitting the Rock
of Gibraltar at full run.

C.G. collapsed, off balance, but was kept from falling to the
floor by Drake's powerful arms that captured her against his
chest, one arm around her waist, the other over her shoulder.
As he saved her, he also stepped on her right foot. Hard.

"Ow," she howled.

"C.G., I'm sorry." His expression was stricken as he leaned
back and gaped down at the foot she was holding gingerly off
the floor. "Are you okay?"

C.G. put her weight on the throbbing foot, but it gave way,
leading her to clutch Drake's arms for support.

Then she was up in his arms, and he was carrying her toward
her office.

Shocked, her breath taken away, she saw the smirk of delight
on Dottie's face as well as the amazed expressions on the faces
of every teller on duty.

"Put me down," she ordered Drake. "You're making a spec-
tacle of us both."

"Who cares? I'm getting you to a chair."

"There are chairs in the lobby."

"Too public. I need privacy to assess the damage."

"Are you a doctor?"

"EMT. I've had training."

That shut her up and she relaxed in his arms, a little, but not
too much. She didn't want to enjoy the ride, after all.

&

When they arrived in her office, Drake eased her effortlessly
down on the chair behind her desk, and C.G. couldn't help

admiring his strength that had gotten her this distance without his even being out of breath. Obviously his physical activities involved more than plunging papers in and out of a briefcase.

Once she was settled, he sank to one knee and gently removed her low-heeled shoe. His hands on her foot, and the sensation they created, almost took C.G.'s mind away from the very real pain she still felt.

"I don't think it's broken," Drake said, his fingers light in their examination. He gave her a reassuring gaze. "Wiggle your toes."

She did.

"Good." His eyes found hers. "Pretty toes."

C.G. tried to pull away from him, but he wouldn't let her go. "Can you move your ankle? Rotate your foot in a circle?"

She did, slowly, but winced as she did.

"Good girl. You're probably all right, but you could have a hairline fracture. Watch it the next few days for swelling or turning black and blue. For now, let's get it elevated, and we need some ice—"

"I'll get it." It was Susie Black, wide-eyed and beautiful, with an adoring smile on her bright-red lips. "We have some in the freezer in the kitchen." Her long, false eyelashes floated down to her cheeks, but Drake didn't seem to notice the seductive gesture.

"Thanks, Susie," he said, barely looking at her, even when she sashayed out the door with considerable movement in her lower region.

"Is all this really necessary?" C.G. questioned when Drake moved another chair in front of her and carefully placed her foot on it, which did make it feel better, she had to admit.

"Absolutely. I want you to rest it for at least a half hour."

"A half hour? Drake, I have work to do."

"Which can wait."

C.G. threw him an incredulous look. "Did I hear that out of your own mouth—saying work can wait?"

"You may never hear it again."

"That's what I thought."

"Special people demand special consideration." His eyes were almost smokey when he gazed at her, and C.G. blinked under their scrutiny, then looked at the wall. She was having little control over the effect he had on her.

Susie returned with a plastic bag of ice cubes and a towel, which Drake took from her, wrapped together, and delicately placed on top of C.G.'s foot, kneeling down beside her again.

"There, how does that feel?" He looked at her with such caring and concern, C.G. almost forgot to answer, and when she did, her voice was breathless, "Fine, thanks."

"Good. You just rest."

"Is there anything else I can do?" Susie asked, leaning over to peer at C.G.'s foot, her long, silky hair brushing Drake's shoulder.

"Not for now, thanks," he answered her.

"You just come get me if there is."

"I will."

C.G. felt like throwing up.

After Susie left, Drake said, "I'm sorry I was in the wrong place at the wrong time."

She gave him a tiny scowl. "You were supposed to wait in my office."

"I got bored when you were gone long enough to handwrite those phone bills for the last two years."

"So you went for coffee."

"Yep."

"Was it good, or was it the company you craved?"

His surprised look almost made C.G. grab her letter opener and cut her tongue out. Her question had had just enough edge to it to make her sound jealous of Susie Black, and the look of amusement that danced in Drake's eyes made her want to evaporate on the spot.

"The coffee was too weak, actually. I prefer it stronger." His mouth twisted upward in an infuriating grin.

Is he only talking about coffee, or is this his assessment of Susie Black as well? C.G. wondered. Not many men could ignore her considerable physical charms. Would that be enough to satisfy a man like Drake Forrest? She didn't know him well enough to know yet. Yet.

He stood up and loosened his tie. "I'm going to get you some aspirin," he said, and was out of the office before C.G. could tell him she had some in her desk. She watched him go straight to Susie who gave him a magnificent smile, two aspirins and a cup of cold water, in that order.

Drake brought the aspirin back to C.G., concerned that she was more injured than she was letting on, and he berated himself for his clumsiness in causing the accident.

"I really am sorry about hurting you," he said, standing beside her desk, watching her, noting the gentle flush on her cheeks and that her hands shook when she put the cup of water down. It would take a few minutes for the aspirin to work.

"Please don't worry about it. I should have looked where I was going." Her smile was generous, and sincere, and Drake found himself more and more drawn to her.

There were two sides to C.G. Grady—the professional businesswoman who was sophisticated, capable, and conscientious, and the devout Christian, willing to give up her lunchtime to bring comfort to someone else and brave enough to have a Bible on her desk.

He'd spotted the Bible the first time he'd walked into her office, and had wondered if she were one of those Christians who witnessed easily of her faith. He admired that, for it had never been easy for him to do.

If she asks about my own beliefs, what will I tell her? he pondered, knowing his spiritual life was far from active at the moment.

"Oh, Mr. Forrest?" He heard the sound of Susie's tight, short skirt swishing over stockinged legs before he saw her, returning with a gigantic ceramic cup with a football logo on it.

"I made some more coffee," she said, in her little girl's voice. "This is stronger. I hope you'll like it."

With eyebrows raised in surprise, Drake took the mug from her long, slender fingers tipped with scarlet polish, and tasted the liquid.

"It's just right," he sighed after a long drink, and was given a woman's smile far different from the one he'd just received from C.G. "Did you bring some for Miss Grady?"

The come-hither smile on Susie's lips died, and she didn't even look at C.G. when she said, "No, I didn't." She made no move to correct her oversight.

"I'd appreciate it if you would."

"Well, okay."

She oozed out of the office and Drake turned to C.G. and shrugged his shoulders. He wanted to tell her that Susie Black meant nothing to him. How could she? She wasn't real.

Instead, he sat down, loosened his tie, and said. "Thoughtful girl." It was all he could think of to say.

"Isn't she," C.G. agreed, thinking how much more human Drake Forrest looked with a cup of coffee in his hand and his tie loosened. Either the caffeine or the effect of Susie had taken the edge off his voice, and C.G. felt his male charisma even from the distance he was sitting from her, and wished she didn't find him so appealing.

seven

Drake looked at his watch. "Only another few minutes and then we'll see how your foot is doing."

"I'm sure it will be fine," C.G. insisted.

"Let's hope. In the meantime, tell me, did you find the information we need?"

C.G. took a long sip of the lukewarm coffee Susie had reluctantly brought her, and wondered where in heaven's name Dottie was. Had she found James?

"The file will be here in a minute," she told him.

"A minute?"

"Yes. Dottie's taking care of it."

Drake gave her a long, silent assessment that made her nervous, as though he were reading her mind and knew she hadn't the foggiest notion where that important file was.

Needing to do something to break the spell of his gaze, she called James Wyatt's number and left a message on his voice mail to come to her office as soon as he got back to his desk. Where was that man anyway?

Turning her attention back to Drake, she said, "Since you must have other things to do, why don't I call you as soon as I have what you want."

She thought he'd agree and leave, but he didn't. Instead, he leaned forward on the chair, resting his elbows on his knees, his hands clasped loosely in front of him, those powerful hands with a sprinkling of blond hairs on their backs, and, after looking at her long enough to give her a thorough case of nerves, said gently, "Where's the file, C.G.?"

She gulped, looked around the office, out in the lobby, up at the ceiling, anywhere but at Drake Forrest. She had just discovered another of his attributes: dogged determination, an admirable trait, to be sure, but not when she was the one being dogged.

His silence demanded she finally bring her attention back to him, which she did, to his eyes, which forcefully held her gaze so she could look nowhere else. "The file. . .is. . ."

"Not here," another voice, breathless from rushing, finished her desperate sentence, and C.G. looked up to see James Wyatt stumbling into the office.

"James, just the man I need," she cried, leaping to her feet before she remembered her injured foot, which reacted to being bounced upon by shooting pain clear to her kneecap.

"Ow," she groaned, falling back into the chair.

In a second Drake was kneeling before her, concern contorting his face while his hands protectively enfolded her injured foot. "Are you all right?" he asked anxiously, to which question C.G. closed her eyes to will away the pain before she opened them again and said, "Dandy."

She also managed to see that James' hands were empty, and her heart sank. Either he didn't have the file, or Dottie hadn't gotten hold of him yet to tell him about it.

James' eyes bulged. "What happened, C.G.?" He leaned forward to watch this stranger's hands on the foot of the woman he had, at one time, adored.

"I had an accident," C.G. explained simply.

"The accident was me." Drake explained further, standing after getting a reassuring nod from C.G. that she was all right.

"I ran into him," C.G. went on. "Didn't see him there."

"Didn't see him?" James questioned, looking up at the tall hunk of a man, the breadth of whose shoulders equalled twice that of his own. *Who is he anyway*? he wondered. He didn't know him. "Sorry I was out of the office when you needed me, C.G. Dottie told me you want the phone bills file."

"Yes, we thought you might have it." C.G. wished Drake Forrest had gone away, so he wouldn't know now that her department could not keep track of a simple file.

"I don't."

"Oh. Well, in that case. . ."

"But I know where it is."

"Fine." Her spirits soared. "Would you please bring it to me right away." She looked straight at Drake, her "problem" solved.

"I don't have it."

C.G.'s eyes traveled slowly to James. "Where is it then?"

Her assistant nervously began swaying from one side to the other, like a teenager about to make a dreaded speech. "In Blue Ridge."

"Blue Ridge?" Her voice was half an octave higher than usual. "How did the file get there?"

"I gave it to Gwen Johnson yesterday. She was here."

"Who's Gwen Johnson?" Drake interrupted.

"Our branch manager in Blue Ridge," C.G. answered him, then asked James, "Why did you give it to her?" She hoped her tone did not give away the fact that the file should never have left the office.

"Gwen is setting up next year's budget and wanted to figure her communications costs—how much her branch's phone lines will run. Since the information for all the branches is kept here—"

"Yes, but James, you could have made copies for her of what she needed instead of giving her the entire file." C.G. was trying to keep her patience. It was not like James to be casual with bank records.

James began to fidget. "Ordinarily I would have, C.G., but I was totally swamped getting that information out for Drake Forrest, fancy consultant, that he demanded immediately, out of all reason, I might add, as though we have nothing else to do around here but cater to him—"

With a perfectly straight face, Drake took a step forward and thrust out his hand. "By the way, I'm Drake Forrest."

James' face turned crimson.

"Go on, James," C.G. urged him, feeling guilty that she hadn't introduced the men earlier and saved James the humiliation he was now feeling.

"W. . .well," he stammered, his voice barely audible, his eyes downcast, "since on Monday there's a meeting of all the branch managers here, and Gwen said she'd bring the file back then, I thought I'd save myself some time and just give her the whole thing—"

"Couldn't she have made the copies herself, and left the file here?"

James looked at C.G. as though she were a firing squad of one and he the victim.

"She could have," he answered stiffly, "but I made a quick decision and just gave it to her. How was I supposed to know that file was going to become so all-fire important overnight?"

"All right, James." C.G. was surprised at his show of temper. Usually he was utterly emotionless. Of course, having Drake present added to his embarrassment, and she didn't want to hurt his feelings any more. "As long as we have the file back on Monday that will be fine." She gave him a supportive smile which he did not return.

Drake cleared his throat. "I'm afraid it won't be fine," he said.

C.G.'s body jerked and she turned to gape at him. Then, knowing that she and he were about to lock heads, she suggested to James, whose shoulders were drooping despondently, that he go back to work.

"What about the file?" he asked.

"I'll take care of it," C.G. promised, and James left without looking again at Drake.

But C.G. looked at him. In fact, her eyes were sparking and Drake knew they were going to tangle.

"That branch meeting is scheduled for ten Monday morning, Drake," C.G. began, her voice firm, "and then I'll have the information for you."

"That's too late."

"Why?"

She wasn't backing down, and he liked that, liked the fact that she wanted answers, sensible answers. She was not a YES person. She had spunk.

"I need to do a lot of work on this acquisition over the weekend," he explained, "and this information is crucial—now." He paused, then added, "So you'll have to go after that file tomorrow morning first thing."

"I'm sorry, but I can't. I have plans."

"Cancel them."

C.G. took in a breath of surprise. "What difference will another two days make?" she challenged him. "We'll have the file here, in this office, Monday morning—"

"And I will have lost two days' work."

"Two days? Surely you aren't going to give Sunday to this, too?"

"Sunday's the same as any other day to me," Drake informed her. He expected more fireworks, but was surprised when C.G.'s expression softened.

"I'm sorry that's so for you. For me, Sunday is the most important day of the week."

Drake glanced over at C.G.'s Bible on her desk. "Do you spend your entire Sunday in church?" he asked, remembering how, years ago, he had gone both morning and evening to services.

"All but about a half hour when they unlock the doors and let us go for lunch," she replied innocently, and Drake knew he was being teased.

"All right, all right, I deserved that."

"Yes, you did, because whether I go once, twice, or all day, it's because I want to. It's exhilarating to be in God's house, worshiping."

"Why?"

"It's where the Power is. The Source I need to keep me energized. It's where the Knowledge is to help me live my life day after day. And the people are wonderful. As close as any family. We care about each other. Take care of each other."

"But can't a person still be a good Christian and not go to church?"

"I suppose, but why would one not want to go? It's only for a few hours a week compared with all the other hours we give to ourselves."

"The Bible says *we* are the temple of God and His Spirit dwells in us?"

It pleased him to see the surprise register on her face.

Somehow it was important that she know he was not a total heathen.

"You know the Scripture," she stated.

"Sure. I grew up with it, read it, studied it. I've even taught Sunday school."

"Do you still do those things?"

"I read the Bible every once in a while, but I don't have time for church."

"Don't *take* time, you mean."

Her statement was not one of condemnation, but of fact.

"That's right. But I'm definitely a believer. I still pray."

"When you can."

"Yes."

"You must be starving then," she said, her eyes dancing with life.

"Starving?"

"A big man like you has to eat food to stay alive. Right? Well, a Christian has to have sustenance to stay spiritually alive." Her expression was kind. "I'm glad we're both Christians, Drake. That will make our working together even nicer."

Drake's sensitivity deflated when she didn't preach at him about what he "should" be doing, and he felt a stab of authentic guilt, knowing they were miles apart on the importance they placed on living the daily life of a Christian. While it obviously meant a lot to C.G., to him, it hadn't been a meaningful part of his life for years, and no one was to blame for that but himself, and his ambitions.

"I think you'd better call Gwen Johnson about that file," he said, wanting to change the subject. He was uncomfortable with the searching way her eyes were focused on him. "Tell her we'll pick it up tomorrow."

"We?"

"Yes. I'm going with you."

eight

C.G. gasped. "It really isn't necessary for you to go with me to Blue Ridge. It won't take long to find the information I need."

"I'm going, too." The words were gentle, but had the finality of an iron door clanking shut.

"To hold my hand?"

He gave her a long, steady look. "Does it need holding?"

C.G.'s cheeks flamed, first at the thought of holding hands with Drake Forrest, then with the realization that that's not what he meant at all. He was just letting her know he thought her incapable of accomplishing the simplest of tasks.

"It's a long ride there, into the mountains," she told him stiffly. "Over two hours."

"No problem. While I'm there I can check out that branch's network interface and get their circuit identification numbers. I'll have to do that with every branch."

"So you'll know which one to disconnect?"

"Yes."

"Can't the branch manager tell you?" She wasn't at all thrilled with the idea that he wanted to go with her.

"There are usually so many circuits—one for data, another for business lines, burglar alarm, automatic teller machines, and a half dozen other things—most managers haven't a clue which is which."

"I see." C.G. took up the phone and started to dial a number, then stopped. "Do you always work seven days a week?"

"If there's a job that needs to be done, yes. And to answer your next question, no, I am not a workaholic."

"Working seven days a week is giving a good imitation of one."

"I work hard, but I'm not obsessed with work. It's the thrill of meeting a challenge head-on, and conquering it, that gives me energy, that drives me. . .relentlessly is a good word, to complete whatever project I'm on."

"So, the struggle means more than the accomplishment?"

"Exactly. Haven't you ever felt that way? Been particularly proud when something you've worked on, grappled with, turns out well?"

C.G. put the phone down and looked at Drake with new understanding. "Yes, I have felt that way, a few times," she admitted, "and I admire your dedication to excellence, Drake. But a man needs more in his life than work."

He leaned back in his chair. "I have more of just about anything I want because of the success I've garnered."

"Fine. When was the last time you took a vacation, with good friends or family?"

A deep frown furrowed his brow, and C.G. picked up the phone, dialed the number of the Blue Ridge branch, and waited for the connection to be made. "Gwen Johnson, please."

From the corner of her eye she saw Drake stand up and begin a thorough examination of her office.

His eyebrows raised when he saw two bronze plaques commending her on career accomplishments.

He leaned closer to peer at a watercolor of a seashore she had painted herself four years before while on vacation at St. Simons Island.

Then he picked up from her credenza the only personal picture in the room, one of her and her parents, on a sailboat, the wind whipping her hair back, all three of them laughing into the wind. The frown, which he'd had all this time, deepened, and when he set the picture down with a thud, she guessed it had been a long time since he'd had a vacation with someone he loved.

Gwen's secretary came on the line and told C.G. that Gwen was on a long distance call but knew she was waiting and would be with her as soon as she could.

"Thank you," C.G. said, and passed the information on to Drake who came over to her desk and sat down on one corner of it, one foot firmly on the ground, the other hanging.

"I promised Georgia National I'd have this project completed in time for the acquisition to take place by December 15. That's only four months, C.G."

"Perhaps that was an unrealistic promise."

"Not at all. I can do it."

"Why the rush?" she asked, piqued.

"GNB needs a tax write-off *this* year."

Their gazes locked, and held, and all sound in the bank disappeared.

"So, where are the pictures of your children?" Drake broke the tension between them. Even though she'd told him she wasn't married, a woman her age sometimes had several children.

"I have none," C.G. answered.

"Boyfriend?" Drake remembered asking this question before, and receiving no answer. He wanted to know more about her private life. The vacation picture of her and her parents bothered him, first, because he couldn't remember the last time he'd had a fun day of sailing, which he enjoyed, and second, he couldn't remember the last time he had been with his parents when the three of them had been laughing.

A sudden envy of C.G. and her family made his throat go dry. His folks were terrific people, yet he spent very little time with them.

Before C.G. could answer his question about her having a boyfriend, Gwen came on the line and they spoke a few minutes.

C.G. put her on hold and told Drake, "The file's at her home but she's not finished with it. She wants to keep it till Monday."

"What's the earliest we can use it at her house tomorrow?"

"Do you mean before or after the sun rises?" C.G. quipped, and Drake worked hard not to laugh.

"See if nine o'clock is okay," he suggested, and C.G.'s look was not endearing as she nodded slightly and asked Gwen the question.

A moment later she put down the phone and said, "Nine o'clock will be fine. She offered us breakfast, but I assured her we would eat before we got there."

"We will?"

"Yes, you at your house, I at mine."

"Oh." She was letting him know she didn't intend to spend one minute longer than necessary in his company.

"I'll pick you up at your house tomorrow at seven," Drake said. "Then you can tell me about your boyfriend."

"Why don't I meet you here at the bank instead, and not tell you anything about the men in my life."

"Men?"

"Figure of speech."

"Is your house on the way to Blue Ridge?" he asked.

"Well, yes."

"Then it's better I pick you up there." He smiled. "You'll have more time for breakfast then."

C.G. knew he was right, but she also knew she wasn't sure she should let him know where she lived. He'd probably come banging on her door at four in the morning, forcing her to get up to accomplish something for The Acquisition.

"I really think meeting here would—"

"Waste time, C.G., and we don't have an unlimited supply of that with this project. Don't worry that I'll come banging on your door at four in the morning to force you to do something for this acquisition."

C.G. gaped at him.

"What's the matter?" he asked.

She was not about to tell him he had just read her mind, but all her senses were heightened, as though she were preparing for mortal combat.

This man was like no other she had ever met: determined, single-minded, brilliant, and so downright attractive she was afraid to spend too much time with him, but she could hardly humiliate herself by letting him know that. Driving to Blue Ridge and back was not going to be easy.

"You'd better pick me up at quarter to seven," she said. "If we take Highway 60 to Blue Ridge, you won't go much over 35 or 40."

"I drive fast, remember?"

"Not on this road, you won't."

She wrote out directions to her house and handed it to him, almost reluctantly, and Drake wondered why. Then a thought came to him. "Did you have plans for tomorrow?" He should have asked her before. Even for him, his attitude had been heavy-handed, and he wouldn't blame her for being miffed.

"As a matter of fact, yes, I did have plans."

"Hopefully you'll be back in time." He wanted to see a smile on her face.

"Afraid not. The singles group from our church is going to Barnsley Gardens. It's an all-day trip."

"With lots of walking?"

"Yes."

"Then it's a good thing you're not going."

"What?"

"Your foot." He pointed to it. "You don't want to overdo so soon after an accident. Being with me will help your foot to heal."

"That's only fair, I suppose, since you're the one who crushed my foot to begin with."

Drake didn't need a billboard to tell him C.G. was not thrilled to be working on Saturday, and that disappointed him about her. He'd given more weekends to his career than he'd stayed home or vacationed. If a job needed doing, then he did it. No complaining. No pouting. That was why more people weren't successful at their occupation—because they wouldn't make the total commitment needed to be the best at what they did. And being the best was right at the top of Drake's intentions.

Maybe he was being a jerk to make C.G. work on Saturday, and give up some activity at her church, but nothing was more important than this acquisition, not even C.G. Grady's social life.

Besides, he wanted to be with her.

nine

C.G. did not want to go to Blue Ridge with Drake, and the reason was simple: It was the weekend, and she had other plans.

When a little voice inside her head suggested she was attracted to the man, made weak by his very look, and wasn't sure how well she would handle being with him in the close confines of his sports car for several hours, she tried to deny it. "I admire his intelligence," she argued out loud with the voice while standing at the closet, contemplating what outfit to wear the next day, "and respect his success. That's it."

Her hand reached for an avocado cotton jumpsuit and she held the gauzy thing in front of her to see if it would do for a special occasion.

Special occasion? Being forced to drive over two hours to do work on Saturday that could be done just as well the following Monday, with a man who was a tyrant, a slave driver, a man too dedicated to his work, a man who had little sympathy for mistakes made? Special occasion?

She slammed the jumpsuit back among the other clothes, and her lower lip jutted out. She was not at all happy she'd had to cancel going with the singles from church to Barnsley Gardens, just to work.

Her eyes flitted over her considerable wardrobe, stopping at a conservative brown skirt, examining a practical white linen dress. Wrong, both of them.

She reached again for the jumpsuit whose material was soft, supple, and feminine. The color was perfect for her red hair, and for the long day ahead, it would be comfortable and sophisticated when a fine gold necklace and earrings completed the ensemble.

Will he like it, though? she wondered, then groaned and glared at the person glaring back at her from the full-length mirror she

51

stood in front of.

The phone rang, and C.G. was surprised that it was Jeffrey Brandon, a young youth minister she had met at a retreat three months before, in St. Augustine, Florida, where he lived and served with a large, affluent church. They'd spent some time together those few days, discovering mutual interests, the most important one being their shared faith.

Since then, he'd called her several times and they'd had nice conversations. He'd sent her a birthday card.

"C.G., I'm on my way to a week-long conference in Gatlinburg, Tennessee and will be going through Cheston Saturday afternoon. I'd like to see you. Maybe for dinner?"

C.G. didn't hesitate. "Sounds wonderful, Jeffrey."

"Good. What time should I pick you up?"

C.G. thought about her trip with Drake to Blue Ridge. She would surely be back no later than three o'clock which would give her plenty of time to shower and change for dinner with Jeffrey.

"How about six o'clock?"

"Great. I'll see you then. You pick a place you'd like to go."

"Do you like barbecued ribs?"

"Sure."

"All right, then dress casual. I'll look forward to seeing you again, Jeffrey." And she would.

While she had dated a number of men both before and after her engagement to Randolph, there had not been any, other than her miscreant fiancé, with whom she would have wanted to spend the rest of her life.

Not that she was all that interested in getting married any more. It seemed every way she turned, she saw men who put career above all else, including family and God. Better to be single, she'd just about decided, than have a husband in name only.

She gave Jeffrey directions to the house, doing so easily since she'd just done the same for Drake who was coming from the same direction.

How different the two men were: Jeffrey was dark-haired, 32, five foot nine, stocky of build, and a man of considerable intellect who thought deeply and spoke slowly. Moved slowly, too, to the point of being indecisive.

Drake, on the other hand, was tall, blond, and definitely decisive. 'Though he drove fast, and acted quickly, there was nothing about his personality that hinted at rashness or recklessness.

He was a man determined to be in control of every situation, who knew exactly what he wanted to do and when. Slow was not in his vocabulary, she was sure.

C.G. stopped the comparison there, choosing not to think how Drake speeded up her pulse while Jeffrey only made her comfortable.

&

In the Great Room of his apartment that night, Drake took from his briefcase some papers that C.G. had given him at the bank. It was only eight o'clock, so he figured he could spend a couple of hours going over them, then hit the shower and go to bed. He wanted to be wide awake tomorrow for the work that was to be done, and for C.G. Grady.

He was uncommonly looking forward to going into the mountains, to Blue Ridge. Since moving from California to Georgia three years before, he had been single-minded in pursuing his career and had learned little about the uniqueness of his newly-adopted state. Tomorrow would be an education in the north Georgia mountains as well as a chance to accomplish some business.

Throwing himself down on the wide, leather sofa, he stretched long, muscular legs over its seven-foot length. Wearing khaki shorts and a matching tank top, he had freedom of movement, which he enjoyed after the confines of a business suit, shirt, and tie.

For the briefest of moments he thought about wearing something similar for the trip the next day, but then thought, *No, I'll be on business, not a date.*

A date? With C.G. Grady? Now there was a thought to wake up a man.

He reached for a cold glass of iced tea from the coffee table beside him and held it firmly in both hands as an image of C.G. came to mind, not that it was ever far since the first moment he'd seen her, walking toward him across the lobby of the bank.

There was something about her that captured his attention, and wouldn't let it go. She was no more beautiful than a half dozen other women he knew, nor more intelligent than they. Witty? Yes, with a saucy sense of humor and an intriguing sparkle in her eyes.

What was it that she had that the other women in his life had not, that made him determined to get to know her better?

He was honest enough with himself to know that the main reason he wanted to go with C.G. to Blue Ridge was to be with her. She could have gotten the file herself; he could have done his work alone at another time. But he wanted to spend time with her, see what she was like outside the office.

He knew it wasn't always wise to have a relationship with someone you worked with, but he'd never met anyone quite like C.G. Grady. He was drawn to her in a way that was disquieting as well as exciting.

With renewed energy, he began shuffling through the papers he'd spread out on the coffee table.

Finding that one was missing, he got up and went to his briefcase, rummaged through files, and that's when he found the letter he'd received that morning from his mother. He'd tossed it into his briefcase, thinking he'd find a minute or two to read it during the day, maybe at lunch. Only he'd taken C.G. to lunch, and after that his mind had been on her and not on his mother's letter.

He slit open the envelope, the same stationery she'd used for the last letter—white parchment. Again, there was a single sheet of paper. What was written on it this time was different, though, from the other:

sophisticated
college graduate with degree in marketing/management,
comes from an old, respectable Georgia family
sings solos in church

Now he laughed, out loud, read the qualifications again, and called his mother, the matchmaker.

"You might as well give up, Mother, because I'm not interested in meeting this 'perfect' woman, whoever she is."

"Drake, won't you even give her a chance?"

"No."

"No?"

"Pretty lady, I appreciate what you're trying to do for me, and I'm sure this woman is terrific, but I want to find my own wife."

"I've already found her."

"Mother. . ."

"She's perfect for you."

"No one's perfect."

"She is."

"Mother. . ."

"All right."

"All right, what? You'll stop your campaign?"

"For the moment."

Drake growled deep in his throat, recognizing that stubborn, determined streak in his mother, from which he got his own. He couldn't be angry with him, for he knew she only wanted what was best for him.

What frustrated him, though, was that she just didn't realize that mothers and sons look at women with entirely different eyes. He wondered if ever, in the history of the world, there had been a successful love match arranged by a mother for her son. He doubted it.

He adored his mother, and would do anything in the world for her—but not this. A man had to choose his own woman.

"Let's change the subject," she suggested cheerfully, and he knew the furrows on her brow had relaxed. "Can you come for dinner tomorrow night? Your father isn't feeling well, and a visit with you would cheer her up."

"What's the matter with Dad?" His father had always enjoyed robust health.

"General malaise. I don't think it's anything serious, dear. He just works too hard in the garden. Thinks he should have the strength and vigor of a twenty-year old."

Drake chuckled. "As far as I'm concerned, he does. I've worked with him. His energy is phenomenal."

"I agree. Anyway, I'm going to fix his very favorite meal, beef stew, and if you come, I'll bake you a pumpkin pie."

"Mom, after all these years being married to Dad, you still want to make him happy. You baby him. And me."

"You're both worth it," Katherine Forrest insisted, and Drake felt the love in her voice.

"I'll be there, Mom, tomorrow night."

"Good."

"What time?"

"Six?"

"See you then."

He hung up reluctantly, not wanting to sever connections with this woman who cared so deeply about him and his father, and others as well.

From the time he'd been a small boy, he had seen her compassion for those who needed her, whether a neighbor, a relative, someone from church, or a stranger who had no one else to turn to.

He couldn't help comparing her with the women he'd been dating lately.

Claudia was a successful attorney who was a killer in court. She was smart, and clever, but when she spoke of her clients, they were just cases, not real feeling, breathing people. He'd dated her only six weeks before tiring of her icicle personality.

Genevieve owned her own accounting firm, but while she was remarkably beautiful, that was her best asset. She was as humorless as the numbers she dealt with day after day. Their relationship had lasted four weeks.

Was it a generational thing? Were women his age too intent on building their careers to respond to the needs of others? Neither Claudia nor Genevieve had ever baked him a pumpkin pie, even though they had learned it was his favorite and he had taken them to many restaurants and even cooked for them in his apartment. They hadn't cared that he loved pumpkin pie, especially homemade.

He picked up the sheet of paper his mother had sent him and stared at it. She liked this woman. Should he give her a chance?

No. He tossed it into his briefcase, intending to take it to the office and put it with the other one. There was no way he was going to give in to his mother's matchmaking. It wouldn't work. He knew it wouldn't work. But he couldn't throw away her loving attempt either.

ten

C.G. was disgusted with herself for forgetting to pick up her mail at the post office, and though it was after nine o'clock, she put on a pair of jeans and a short-sleeved blue blouse and drove the five minutes, unlocked her post office box and reached inside.

There was only one envelope, from her mom. She smiled but did not open it until she got outside and into her car where she started the engine and felt the relief of the air conditioning. August in the South was a constant battle against heat and humidity, and she let the motor idle as she read,

> *great personality*
> *highly intelligent*
> *a little rough around the edges*
> *adorable*
> *protective*

C.G. felt guilty that she'd forgotten to call her mom when she'd gotten the first teaser. She really did appreciate all her parent's efforts to make her life more interesting.

She studied the words again, then suddenly laughed out loud as she figured out what was going on. Two minutes after going through the front door of her house she called her mom who answered on the third ring.

"I know who 'he' is, Mom," C.G. enthused.

"How could you, Chryssie?" Jane Grady responded, "when I haven't given you his name?"

C.G. chuckled softly, first of all because her mom refused to call her C.G., which initials she used in business because they sounded far more sophisticated than Chrysanthemum Geraldine, and secondly because she was pleased with herself for having figured out the mystery before having to ask her mom to explain it to her.

"Names don't matter," she said. "It's what he is that's important, right?"

This strong, dependable, adorable, mischievous, rough-around-the-edges, protective, wavy blond-haired creature with a great personality had to be—A DOG, a cocker spaniel, no doubt.

About a month ago, her mom had expressed concern that she must be lonely, living by herself in a house out in the country, without anyone to share it with. "You need a dog. For protection and companionship."

"I don't need a dog, Mom," C.G. had tried to assure her. "I'm fine here by myself."

"Your father is concerned about you."

"I appreciate that—"

"And so am I, so we have an idea how to fill the emptiness in your life."

"There isn't an emptiness, Mom."

Her argument had not changed her mother's mind, obviously, since now she'd received two notes describing just the animal her parents thought she needed.

Well, maybe it wouldn't be so bad to have a pooch to come home to, a loving, warm body to snuggle up to and tell my problems to after a hard day at the bank.

"I hope you'll like him, Chryssie," Jane Grady went on.

"It may not be a case of whether or not I like him, Mom, but whether or not I'll have time for him. I'm not home very much."

"He'll understand."

"But I don't want him to be lonely when I'm gone."

"He's used to being alone, dear."

"I'm just not sure I'm ready for that kind of commitment."

"I wouldn't worry about that until you've been around him awhile."

"But that's just the trouble, Mom. If he's as adorable and protective as you say, I'll fall in love with him for sure."

"That's the whole idea, Chryssie."

"Mom, I want to meet him before I make any promises to love him for the rest of his life."

"Of course, dear. That goes without saying."

"Is he at your house now?" C.G.'s curiosity was growing.

There was a pause before Jane Grady responded. "No, he's not, but I'll call you as soon as I can arrange for him to be."

"Tell me one thing more, Mom. Is he big or small?" C.G. was sure they were talking about a cocker spaniel.

"Oh, he's big, dear. Very big."

C.G. frowned. She'd have to get out her dog encyclopedia and see what other blond, wavy-haired breed there was. An Airedale, perhaps? "Is he too big for my house?" she asked, not wanting the animal to feel confined.

"Time will tell," came the ambiguous reply.

"I have to go, Mom, but thanks for caring. I'm glad we're talking about a dog here, and not a man, because if you were trying to set me up with a man, my answer would be NO! You know how I feel about matchmaking."

"Yes, I do."

"Remember Sandra Bishop? Her parents found her the perfect husband and they got married and then divorced within six months."

"I remember, Chryssie, and that was sad. Well, I'll talk to you soon, dear." Her mother hung up, almost quickly, C.G. thought.

She felt lighthearted all of a sudden. The idea of getting a dog had taken her mind off Drake Forrest, the threat he posed to her career, and the even more immediate threat he posed to her sensibilities. Tomorrow wasn't far off.

❧

The day didn't start out to be a disaster, it just ended that way.

At quarter to seven in the morning, when Drake knocked on C.G.'s door, the sun was bright, the clouds were clear, and C.G. climbed into his black Corvette with a sense of optimism that nothing would go wrong today that would tarnish her business reputation in his eyes.

"I'd never been in a Corvette before until you drove me to

lunch," she told Drake as she settled into the contoured seat and put her purse on the floor by her feet. "It's fabulous." *And intimate,* she could have added—just two seats, and a small cargo space behind them.

The high-backed bucket seat enfolded her in a private world that included only one other: the driver, whom she could touch without even stretching out her arm.

Her eyes traveled over the luxurious red interior; her fingers touched the deeply-grained leather upholstery.

She'd often heard that a car mirrored the owner, and in this case, it was certainly true: This magnificent machine of power and class *was* Drake Forrest.

Drake turned the key in the ignition, and brought the mighty engine to life.

"I'll bet this car is fast," C.G. said.

"Sure is. Zero to sixty in—"

"Don't tell me," C.G. interrupted, her eyes noting the words "air bag" on the dash in front of her. That should have helped her breathe easier, but for some reason it didn't.

When Drake stepped on the accelerator, they zoomed down the narrow, tree-lined country road, and C.G. swallowed hard. She was not a speed freak.

"Do you know exactly how to get to Gwen's?" he asked. "We don't want to get lost."

"And lose valuable time."

"Time is money."

"Yes, but there are more important things."

He threw her a serious look. "Name one. Without money the world does not move. Deny that."

"I can't. Of course money is necessary, but there's the inner man to consider, too."

"Which sounds like too serious a conversation for this ride."

C.G. accepted Drake's closing of that topic, but she hoped, in the months they'd be working together, that he'd share something of his spiritual life with her.

Why people did or did not follow the Lord was fascinating to her. She loved to talk about it, with anyone she met, and she prayed every day that she'd be an effective witness. Some wonderful experiences had come her way.

"I like your outfit," he said, five minutes later.

"I like your shirt."

The truth was, she liked him in his shirt, which was exactly the same color green as her jumpsuit and fit snug across his considerable chest. Like her dress, it was also short-sleeved, exposing his long, muscular arms—

"I hope we don't look like those old married couples who purposely dress alike," he said, unknowingly interrupting her runaway admiration.

"I'm sure no one will take us for that," C.G. murmured, settling herself deeper in the leather seat, all too aware of how easily she could reach out and touch his hand, ruffle his hair . . .she clasped her hands firmly together, on her lap, and squeezed till her knuckles turned white.

Drake was tense. It was all he could do to keep from reaching out and touching C.G.'s hand, or ruffle her hair. His attraction to her was far more than he'd realized, and being only inches apart in the 'Vette didn't help his libido one bit.

No desk separated them here, as it did in her office. No other people looked on, as they could at the bank.

He smelled her perfume, heard more perfectly the lilt in her voice, the gentle Southern accent, and he knew his willpower was going to be put to the test before this trip was over.

Now was the perfect time to find out if she was off-limits. No use tying himself into romantic knots if she was committed to another man. "So, C.G. Grady, are you ready to answer the question I've put to you twice now?"

"What question is that?" she asked him innocently.

"Is there a special man in your life?"

There was a long pause before she answered, "No, there's not."

"I find that hard to believe."

"Thank you." She blushed, and he was amazed. When was the last time he'd seen a woman blush?

Then she caught him off guard by boldly asking, "How about you?"

"Not married. Not engaged," he told her, and stopped himself just in time from saying, "But falling in love," an incredulous thought that had just sailed into his mind.

"Divorced?" she asked.

He laughed then. "Not that either. What other personal information would you like to know about me?" He captured her gaze and held it to his, and the most powerful feeling swept over him, that of a great contest beginning, a battle of wills. He wanted her, and she knew it. She was drawn to him, and he knew it.

"Frankly, Mr. Forrest," she said with considerable verve, "I couldn't care less about your personal life."

Drake laughed heartily, and the boisterous sound reverberated through the Corvette, telling them both that he didn't believe her, and that they had moved to the second stage in their relationship: they were no longer strangers.

eleven

The countryside they traveled through was like a timeless picture, its verdant hills dotted with tall pines and hardwood forests and fat, black cattle grazing by ponds and streams. Houses, set far back from the road, nestled among healthy green grass and flower or vegetable gardens tenderly cared for and abundant in the rich, red clay of Georgia. Occasionally there were two or three long, rectangular chicken houses standing end to end, old and abandoned, their roofs rusted and dilapidated.

Far more present were small brick churches with white shutters, particularly Baptist but sometimes a Methodist or Church of God. They sat on knolls and hills, open land around them, with white steeples pointing to the sky as if to say, "Our Father is in heaven," and they reminded passers-by that people worshiped in this county.

Lying quietly beside most of these churches were graveyards, neatly trimmed and colorful with bouquets of fresh and fake flowers at nearly every headstone.

C.G. pointed out to Drake various scenes of interest, but neither of them were forgetting his lengthy laughter over her assertion that she didn't care a whit about his personal life. They knew the mood had changed between them. They chatted amiably about serious things, and not so serious things. They laughed together. They were silent at times, enjoying the sunbright summer scenery.

Then, about halfway to Blue Ridge, C.G. realized what was happening: she was enjoying herself, with him. It had to stop. She did not want to be his friend. Well, not his *good* friend. They would be working together for many months to come, and she absolutely was not going to get involved with him, even though every part of her was effected by Drake Forrest's very presence.

They took a corner marked 30 miles per hour at 45, and C.G., who found herself nearly in Drake's lap, complained, "Does everyone from California drive fast?" He'd told her he'd grown up there, and graduated from a university in Southern California.

"Am I going too fast?"

"For me, but obviously not for you." She sighed with relief when the road straightened out and she could sit up.

Drake looked over at her, saw the paleness of her face, and realized only her ladylike demeanor had prevented her from demanding he slow down, which even he now knew he should do on this winding two-lane country road.

They were approaching an old building on the left labeled Smith's General Store, and Drake pulled onto a graveled parking lot and stopped the car.

The store looked like it had stood on this spot for a hundred years and hadn't received a lick of paint since the original coat. There was rust around the metal door, and windows that one could hardly see through.

"Let's get a soft drink," he suggested, reaching over to touch her hands which were clenched together. Expressionless, she pulled her hands away from him.

Unfastening his seat belt, he gingerly got out of the car and hurried over to C.G.'s side and opened her door. She just sat there until he extended his hand to help her out. For a moment he thought she wasn't going to accept his offer, but then, without looking at him, she put her hand in his and squeezed it for support as she raised herself from the seat.

Her fingers were cold and trembling, and he wasn't egotistical enough to think it was because he was holding them. She was scared. Or sick.

"Are you okay?" he asked, concerned, and feeling guilty.

"No."

"Is your stomach upset?"

"Yes."

"Do you have a headache?"

"Yes."

"You should have told me to slow down a long time ago," he gently chastised her.

"I'm not a back seat driver."

"But you were sitting in the front," he said with a grin. "Do curving roads bother you?"

"Only when I'm the passenger."

"C.G., I'm sorry."

She pushed by him and went into the store and walked straight to an old Coke machine. He followed her. Now there were dapples of perspiration on her upper lip, and he hoped she wasn't going to throw up, although better here than in his 'Vette.

"What do you want?" he asked, fishing change from his pocket.

"A Seven-Up or Sprite, please, and thank you."

"For what? Making you sick?"

The coins dropped down and the machine grumbled as it spat out its possession. Drake opened the can for her and watched, concerned, as she took a small sip. Then another.

What a jerk I am, he thought.

She closed her eyes and shuddered, then slowly opened them and looked at him. Drake stopped breathing. Her eyes, so large and expressive, like fine blue Wedgwood, with a darker rim around the iris, wrapped him in their beauty and captured his heart. He could not and did not want to look away.

In that moment, he knew she was precious to him, that he wanted to take care of her.

"I really do apologize for speeding," he said, wishing he could take her sickness on himself.

She smiled, wanly, and laid a gentle hand on his arm which seared his flesh. "I should have told you how I get. It's my own fault for trying to be brave."

"You are brave."

"Stupid, you mean."

"Wonderful."

Their gaze took on a new depth, a telling to each other that something was happening between them, and Drake put his hand over C.G.'s, which was still on his arm, and leaned closer to her.

She did not move away, and when he kissed her, lightly, not hurriedly, a rush of joy plunged from head to foot, and Drake felt as though this were the first kiss he had ever given a woman. To him, at this moment, it was the first kiss that had real meaning.

He was in love.

"Can I help you folks?" A rough voice from behind them interrupted their tender moment, and Drake glared at the bearded old man for his inexcusable clumsiness in not noticing they were not interested in store merchandise.

"We're fine," Drake said, hating to leave the soft lips he had just enjoyed, hating to allow space to come between him and C.G. With irritation, he jammed some more coins into the ancient Coke machine and waited till it gave him a Classic Coke, his favorite. Then he took a long swig.

"Well, just look around," the man said. "If you don't see what you want, ask for it." He ambled off.

Drake looked at C.G. and was delighted to see she was trying to keep from giggling. She must be feeling better; therefore, he was feeling better, too.

"I think I'll browse a bit," she said. "I'll be ready to go again in a few minutes."

"Take your time," Drake insisted, reaching out to caress her cheek. "We don't have to rush. We won't rush any more today. On this whole trip."

C.G. gave him a You've-got-to-be-kidding look, as though not believing that he was willing to travel at less than warp speed.

"I'm going to check out the fishing gear. I see some over there." He pointed.

"Oh, I'll look too."

"Don't tell me you're a fisherman."

"Absolutely not. I'm a fisherwoman."

Drake chuckled. "I stand corrected."

"My daddy taught me to fish when I was only seven. I have a knack for it."

Drake's eyebrows raised. "A knack?"

"Yes, although sometimes I think it's because I have red hair."

He laughed out loud. "You're putting me on."

"No," she insisted. "Whenever I go out with other people, I always catch fish, even when no one else does. I think, as a redheaded person, I have some unique scent on my hands that fish die for. Literally."

"Now I've heard everything." He placed his hand lightly on the back of her waist and directed her toward the aisle which had shelf after shelf of baits, lures, poles, and accessories.

They examined the merchandise, exchanging comments, and Drake was amazed to find a woman who loved fishing as much as he did, although one would never know it in counting the number of times he'd been in the last five years. Where had his free time gone? Certainly not in fishing.

He remembered seeing a sign a mile or so back which had pointed to the Toccoa River. *Why not buy a bunch of gear and go spend an hour on the bank fishing?* Even before the thought was fully formed in his mind, he knew he wouldn't do it. He had forgotten how to be spontaneous.

"I don't believe your theory, you know," he said to C.G., and she gave him a frown.

"Is that a challenge, Mr. Forrest?"

"Sure is, Miss Grady, if you're not afraid to take it."

"Afraid. Sir, I'll fish you under the dock. Or bank. Or wherever we go to prove my point."

"It's a date."

C.G. took in a quick breath and realized what she'd just agreed to, which she couldn't agree to, and wouldn't.

Hoping Drake would understand, she said gently, "I don't think that's a good idea."

"What isn't? Our fishing together?"

"Our having a date to go fishing."

"Why?"

C.G. put down a package of spinner bait. This was an awkward moment. She knew she would enjoy being with Drake, fishing, or doing absolutely anything at all. She was liking him far more than she should. She had even let him kiss her, which had been a big mistake. She had to stop what was happening right now, before things got out of hand.

"I'd enjoy fishing with you, Drake, but we both know we should not socialize since we have to work together for months. That would inevitably lead to. . .complications."

"Complications," he said reflectively, as if tasting the word in his mouth to see if he liked it or not.

She waited for his reaction, not knowing him well enough to even guess what that might be, but when he began nodding his head up and down, she thought he understood and shared her feelings.

"So you think there will be complications, C.G., if we start dating while we're working together?" he said.

"Yes, don't you?"

"Yep. In fact," and with one hand he cupped her chin and slowly, very slowly, moved his face toward hers, and left a lingering kiss on both her cheeks, "I intend to bring on all the complications I can."

She gaped at him.

"Consider yourself warned, Miss Grady. From this moment on, you're mine."

twelve

Drake walked jauntily out of the store into the bright sunlight, and C.G. stared after him, watching the screen door slam behind him not believing what she'd just heard. She was his? He was staking a claim on her, as though she were a piece of property, with no say in the matter?

The grizzled old man behind the counter kept looking from Drake to C.G., then to Drake, then back to C.G. He knew what was coming, and it didn't take long.

A smoldering surge of adrenalin sent C.G. charging after Drake, where she caught up with him at the front of the car and squarely placed herself in front of him.

With barely controlled anger she said, "I'm warned, am I? I'm yours, am I?" She reached up and tweaked his nose, hard.

"Hey, cut that out."

Her eyes were swirling dark storm clouds. "Do I leap into your arms now, or wait till I'm bidden?"

"Whichever." His grin was devilish.

She reached for his nose again, but his hand caught her wrist. "One bruised nose a day is enough, thanks. Why are you upset?"

C.G. struggled to be free of him, but he wouldn't let her go. "I don't appreciate the fact that *you* have decided I am going to be yours. Don't I have a say?"

"You did. You said we weren't going to get involved because of possible complications."

"And then you said you were going to bring on all the complications you could, and from that moment on I was yours."

"That's about it."

"No, it isn't."

"I know you like me, C.G. You know I like you. So why fight our feelings for each other?"

70

"I need a whole lot more than physical feelings for a man before I enter a relationship."

"What do you need? Whatever it is, I'll give it to you."

He was calm, and sure of himself, and C.G. knew he hadn't a clue what a Christian woman wanted in the man she'd love.

He let her wrist go as she shook her head sadly. "You're not the man for me, Drake."

"Explain why not, when I know you're as attracted to me as I am to you."

"I can't deny the attraction, but I won't foster it."

"Why?"

"Because years ago I learned that there are family men and there are businessmen. You are a businessman. In love with the business. Married to the business. First comes the business, then making money, finally wife and children come in last."

"Aren't you being a little judgmental for only knowing me a few days?"

She tilted her chin up in determination. "I don't think so, from the conversations we've had. I've known your type before."

They stood, staring at each other for long moments while each tried to figure out the other, until C.G. finally decided she was foolish to even be having this conversation. Drake Forrest was just a man used to getting his way, in business as well as with women. What he wanted he took. Well, he would not have her.

"There will never be anything between us, Drake. Now, let's get on to Blue Ridge." She turned sharply and strode to the car and got in.

Drake still stood where he'd been, only now his hands were on his waist and he was staring at her thoughtfully.

"Blue Ridge it is," he agreed, and when he got into the car, he didn't slam the door or say anything harsh to her, which she'd thought he would do.

In fact, his whole demeanor was that of a man who had plotted his course, run into an obstacle, cleared it out of the path, and was on his way again.

When he began to whistle, C.G. got worried. She hadn't said or done a thing to deter him.

"I think there's more to your resistance of me than that I'm a dedicated businessman," he said after five minutes of driving.

"No, I just recognize a workaholic when I see one, and that attitude has already changed your life."

"How so?"

"You don't have time for God because you're too bent on accomplishing."

"So I'm not acceptable because I don't do certain things? I told you I was raised in the church."

"But not attending now."

"I still read the Bible. Do I have to read it so many minutes a day to be a 'real Christian?' I still pray. Do I have to be on my knees at certain times in order to be okay in your eyes?"

C.G. looked at him gravely. "Don't mock my beliefs, Drake."

"Those aren't beliefs, they're traditions. C.G., I'm a decent man. A moral man."

"I'm sure you are." The tone of her voice showed she meant it.

"But that's not good enough for you?"

"It's not a question of your being good enough; it's a question of priorities. I want more than just a good man, a well-intentioned man. I want a man who loves the Lord and His principles as much as I do, and wants to live by those standards every day."

When he did not respond she added, "I think you know what I mean."

He reached for her hand, took it, and held it up to his lips. "Yes, I do know, but that still isn't going to stop me from wanting you."

C.G. took her hand away from him. "It should."

He grinned, his familiar self-confidence surging to the fore once again. "I'm a confident man," he said. "One of two things is going to happen in our future together: either I'm going to learn to put other things before business, and become the sterling Christian man you want, or you're going to change your mind about how important those are in a relationship."

He smiled the challenge over to her and was not expecting her to jab him lightly in the arm.

"There's a third possibility that you've overlooked, Mr. Forrest."

"Oh? What's that?"

"It's that neither of us will change our minds, and we'll go our separate ways."

He almost stopped the car to take her in his arms and kiss that smug look off her mouth. She was so sure of herself, what she wanted from life and a man. Well, they'd see which one of them gave in.

For the rest of the drive to Blue Ridge, they did not raise again the question of their relationship, but they did talk, a little, of unimportant things. Both of them, though, knew a line had been drawn in the sand.

Drake expected C.G. to step over that line and give in to him, regardless of his relentless ambition and lukewarm commitment to God.

C.G. knew she wouldn't, but hoped Drake could, some day, find meaning in a faith that had once been his.

In the meantime, she was wise enough to know she should guard her heart carefully. There was a lot about this man she admired, and probably more she would come to admire if they pursued a personal relationship. Better to close off her feelings right now, before she was involved, rather than later, when real complications could arise.

She tried to relax and enjoy the interesting countryside where people weeded in their front yards or sat in monstrous oak rockers on their front porches and big, scruffy dogs laid out by metal mailboxes at the end of their owners' driveways and watched the traffic, or lack of it, go by in either direction.

They passed antique shops that didn't have a single car parked in front, and old stores that were being swallowed up by that wonder weed of the South, kudzu, which crept up telephone posts, along fences, and over anything else in its relentless path to control its territory, sometimes growing as much as a foot a day.

Gazing over a particularly prolific valley of the leafy, green vine, C.G. started to smile as it suddenly took on the personification of Drake Forrest. Would he give up on her now, because he knew she was serious about not marrying a man wedded to his work, or would he pursue her relentlessly, like the thorny tendrils of the kudzu vine, attempting to claim her despite her resistance, just as the kudzu dominated anything in its way?

She laughed out loud.

"What's so funny?" he asked.

"Kudzu. Just kudzu."

To his puzzled look, she offered no explanation, but she would never look at the stuff again without thinking of Drake Forrest.

Drake wondered if C.G.'s thinking of kudzu had anything to do with him. Failing to see any connection, he was, nonetheless, glad she was in a good mood, not put off by their serious statements of position a few minutes before.

"So," he said, "tell me what C.G. stands for."

C.G. shook her head back and forth.

"State secret, huh?"

"That's right"

"Not even to be revealed to good friends who promise not to tell the news media?"

She turned and mouthed the word NO.

"I want to be your friend, C.G. Grady."

"As well as my sweetheart?"

"Yes, what could be better?"

"One is fine; the other impossible."

He didn't argue with her, but he wasn't changing his plan one bit. He knew a good thing when he saw it, and C.G. Grady was the finest woman he'd met in a month of Sundays.

thirteen

They arrived in Blue Ridge, population 1400, elevation 1750, two hours after they'd started from Cheston, but finding Gwen Johnson's house proved a challenge. She'd obviously left out some part of the directions, and it was when they were turning around to go back the way they'd come that the first disaster struck.

Drake pulled into a long driveway and was starting to back out when C.G. warned, "Be careful of the ditch on either side of the drive. There's tall grass covering it."

"Not to worry," Drake responded cheerfully, looking over his right shoulder. "Everything's under control."

That's when he cut the corner too soon, and the right rear of the Corvette slipped into the ditch.

C.G. cried out, and clutched Drake's arm, thankful that in this intimate car, he was so close. A word slipped out of his mouth that was not one C.G. would have used, but she understood its meaning, and Drake's frustration.

He put the car in forward gear and tried to go ahead, but the right rear of the 'Vette was grounded. They were royally stuck, though not dangerously so, for the ditch was not deep.

Drake got out to assess the damage and assured C.G. she'd be okay if she stayed inside, which she did, dreading to think what might be wrong with his lovely, expensive car. "We'll have to get a tow truck," he yelled from behind the car after a minute's examination. "I'll go up to the house to make the call."

In a minute he was back. "No one's home."

Obviously he was disgusted, but not mad, and C.G. knew why: he was a problem solver. After initial frustration, his orderly mind kicked into gear, attacking the problem, not wasting energy on temper. She liked that.

"I don't see another house on this road," he said, leaning his arms through the open window of the driver's side, "so we'll have to walk."

"We?"

"I won't leave you here alone since I have no idea how far the nearest house is or how long I'll be gone." He gave her a lop-sided grin of contrition. "Sorry about this."

She shrugged. "Accidents happen." She didn't vocalize the fact that in the high heat and humidity, they'd be soaked with sweat in a matter of minutes. Not something to look forward to.

Climbing across the driver's seat, C.G. got out, helped by Drake's strong hands, and the two of them were just starting to walk away when a massive Chevy truck rumbled down the road toward them. Drake waved his arms, the truck stopped, and a big, burly man, carrying more than 200 pounds on a short frame, got out and walked toward them.

"Y'all need some help?" he asked, his deep, gravelly voice matching the two-days' growth of beard on his face.

"Afraid so," Drake answered. "Do you have a chain?"

"Yes, sir. We'll have that baby outa there in a jiffy." His eyes traveled from one end of the gleaming Corvette to the other. "Sure is one fine car."

"That she is."

In less than five minutes the 'Vette was on level ground and Drake was shaking the man's hand. "I can't thank you enough. Your coming along just when you did, here in the middle of nowhere, was a miracle."

"Could be." The big man smiled broadly revealing one miss-ing tooth right in front.

Drake reached for his billfold, but the man stopped his hand. "No need for that, sir." He reached into his own pocket and pulled something out and handed it to Drake. "Have a good one," he yelled, getting back in his truck. He drove away.

C.G. went over to Drake and looked at what the man had given him. It was a pewter cross, small enough to fit in the palm of a hand.

"I didn't even get his name," Drake said quietly, staring at the cross, then down the road toward the truck that had just disappeared over a hill.

All C.G. could think was what a marvelous testimony to leave behind after a work of kindness.

Drake was quiet during the rest of the drive to Gwen Johnson's house, which they found in another few minutes, and C.G. respected that silence, only interrupting it to give directions. But when they finally arrived and parked in the small driveway of the one-story cedar home, Drake said, "I need to get under the car to see if there's anything wrong."

"Oh, I hope nothing is," C.G. responded.

"Me, too, but I won't drive home without checking."

"Of course not. Here comes Gwen."

A tall, slim career woman in her early forties, with short, wavy hair, came out on the front porch and greeted them, her effervescent personality immediately apparent.

"Oh, C.G., I'm sorry to have caused you so much trouble, to make you drive all this way. How do you do, Mr. Forrest; I'm honored to meet you. If there's anything I can do to make your work easier, please let me know. Gracious, isn't this a hot day? Just feel that humidity. Let's go inside."

It was a pretty house, not spacious, but neat, done in peach and blue, the colors repeating themselves in the furniture and accessories. Mostly, it was a cheerful place, with oversized windows that let in lots of Georgia sunshine. And, it was air conditioned, for which both C.G. and Drake were thankful.

"I've put the folder you want to look at on the kitchen table," Gwen told C.G. and Drake, mostly Drake, C.G. noticed, "and I'll busy myself in an office down in the basement. If you need me, just call down the stairs. There's coffee already brewed, and iced tea and soft drinks in the refrigerator. Help yourself. Chocolate chip cookies are in the cookie jar, and I've made tuna sandwiches for lunch—"

"Gwen, Gwen," C.G. stopped her, "you've gone to too much trouble for us."

"It was no trouble at all," Gwen insisted. Turning to Drake she said, "I think it's exciting that we're going to be a part of Georgia National."

"It's a major step," Drake said with a smile that would turn any woman's head. He then explained about their accident.

"How awful," Gwen commiserated. "That beautiful car. Those awful ditches."

"I need to check it out for damage, although I won't know much till I get it jacked up. Let's just hope we can get home tonight."

C.G.'s eyes widened. "You think there's that possibility?"

"Could be."

"Can I help you in any way?" Gwen volunteered. "Hold something?"

"Thanks, I'd appreciate that."

He and Gwen started out the door, but he turned back. "Start without me on those bills, C.G. I'll be in as soon as I can."

C.G. was irritated with herself for not offering to help, too. As she made her way to the table to start her work, she could not help but think how easily Drake gathered women to him: Susie Black at the bank, and now Gwen Johnson.

I am not jealous, C.G. told herself, and she pulled the bills from the file and began her research, but she knew exactly when ten minutes had passed and Drake and Gwen were still not back in the house with word on the damage to the car.

When she heard them laughing outside, it galled her that Drake had been in such an all-fire hurry to get here, get the information, and get home, but now he had enough time to chat and laugh with a woman he'd only just met.

"We're in trouble," Drake called out, as he burst into the house with Gwen following close behind.

C.G. stood up to get the news.

"The oil pan's been ruptured. There's a leak."

"That's bad, isn't it?"

"We don't go anywhere until it's fixed. Hopefully a local garage has another one that'll fit." He turned to Gwen. "Could you recommend a place? Or a mechanic? I want someone good; no weekend hotshot."

"I know just the man," Gwen declared, grinning from ear to ear as though she had just won a million dollars. "Henry Jenkins.

Most folks in town use him. There's nothing he doesn't know about cars."

"Great. Can you give me his number?"

"I'll do better than that, Drake; I'll call him for you myself."

C.G. sat down. *I am not jealous*, she thought, wishing Gwen weren't quite so efficient and already on a first-name basis with Drake.

While he talked to the mechanic about the Corvette, Gwen poured him some iced tea from a large, glass pitcher in the refrigerator, then took from a cookie jar a half dozen plump, chocolate chip cookies and set them on the table with his drink.

C.G. cleared her throat. She was thirsty and hungry.

Gwen giggled. "C.G., I'm sorry. I've overlooked you. What can I get you to drink?"

"Anything diet will be fine."

"Okay."

Gwen fixed her a Diet Dr. Pepper, but didn't give her a plate of cookies. "May I have one of Drake's cookies, Gwen? They look delicious."

"Silly me," Gwen exclaimed. "Of course. Help yourself. I have lots more for the man."

For the man, but not for me, C.G. surmised.

She knew the cookies would be delicious. They were. She knew they would still be warm. They were. She had always liked Gwen Johnson. That might soon change. She stuffed another cookie into her mouth, despite how many calories it contained.

Drake plunked the phone back on its receiver. "Like I said, we're in trouble." He came over to the table and faced the women. "Henry knows he can fix the 'Vette."

"I knew he could," Gwen exclaimed, clapping her hands enthusiastically. C.G. remained quiet.

"The problem is he doesn't have an oil pan on hand at his garage. So, he's going to check Cleveland or Cheston at the dealerships there and if they have one, he'll go pick it up, then come here to put it on."

"Does he think he'll find one?" C.G. asked, seeing what kind of trouble they could be in if Henry couldn't locate just what was needed. It was Saturday. Tomorrow was Sunday and, in most of the surrounding small towns, nearly every business would be closed. They might not get the Corvette fixed till Monday.

Tonight Jeffrey Brandon was taking her to dinner.

The worst problem, of course, was the possibility of spending the night under the same roof as Drake.

"You can have faith in Henry," Gwen declared, putting more cookies on the plate, to replace the ones C.G. had taken, winning for herself Drake's dynamite smile of appreciation. "If he says he'll find one, he will. And if he finds one, he'll work overtime to put it on."

Drake nodded. "That's what he told me."

Gwen sat down in a chair next to him. "But, on the wee chance that the car can't be fixed, you don't have to worry about where to spend the night. You can stay right here."

"Oh?"

"Yes."

C.G. coughed.

"You and C.G., of course."

"How many bedrooms do you have, Gwen?" C.G. asked, sure there was hardly 1500 square feet in the house.

"I have two."

"Two?"

"Two."

C.G. and Drake looked at each other, and she was sure she saw one corner of his mouth raise. *If he thinks I'll spend the night in the same house with him, getting cozy, he has another thing to learn about what kind of a man will win my heart. Certainly not one who has only one thing on his mind.*

fourteen

"Let's cross that bridge when we come to it," Drake suggested.

"Good idea," Gwen agreed, rising. "I'll leave you two to your task. I'll be downstairs if you need me."

After she was gone, Drake said, "Gwen is great, isn't she?" He gobbled down the last chocolate chip.

"A regular lamb," C.G. agreed, her eyes down, trying to concentrate on the pages before her, looking for the designation that would identify an analog line.

She didn't want to think of the fact that not only had she missed going with the singles today, but she might also miss seeing Jeffrey tonight if they couldn't get the car fixed early, not to mention her greatest concern—spending even more time than necessary with Drake Forrest.

Back at Smith's General Store he had made it abundantly clear where he wanted, intended, their relationship to go. Well, he might know his own mind, but she knew her mind as well: there was not going to be a relationship.

It took less time than they'd expected to locate the billing code that identified the number of analog data circuits Ashford Bank and Trust utilized. There were fifteen.

That was more than long enough, however, for Gwen to come back up to the kitchen from her basement office and fix them whopping tuna sandwiches on hoagie rolls for lunch, accompanied by fresh sliced tomatoes and homemade brownies.

At the end of the meal, C.G. was ready for a nap, but opted instead to sit outside on the front porch while Drake called the garage to see how Henry's search for an oil pan was progressing.

When he joined her a few minutes later, from the stern look on his face it was easy to deduce he had not heard what he'd wanted.

"Henry's found the pan," he told her, "but it's in Atlanta and it will be three or four hours before he can get it, come by here, and replace the ruptured one."

His exasperated sigh led C.G. to say, "You're thinking we'll be lucky to get it on today at all, aren't you?"

"Right."

Drake sat down beside her, both feet solidly on the ground, so the swing did not move.

"This is proving to be a costly trip," C.G. said. "You're losing not only a lot of your valuable time, but money for your car as well."

Drake nodded. "That's the truth. Things better go smoother than this from now on, or we'll never get this acquisition sewed up by the end of the year."

"Sure we will," C.G. insisted. "Things like this just happen, that's all."

"Not with me, they don't."

C.G. frowned. "I take it you're saying that with proper planning and careful supervision, problems don't arise."

"Precisely."

"How would you have planned not to back into that ditch that damaged the car?"

He threw her a thoughtful look, then began to smile. He also started the swing moving back and forth. "That was worse than bad planning," he said, "it was just plain dumb driving."

"It was an accident."

"So says the eternal optimist. That's what you are, isn't it?"

C.G. thought for a moment. "I guess so. I much prefer to find a positive solution than wallow in self-recrimination."

Drake chuckled and put his arm around the back of the swing. "No wonder you're different from any woman I've ever known."

"That's a broad statement."

"But true." He turned to face her, his eyes studying her lips. "You *are* different, C.G. Grady. I don't know all the reasons why, yet, but I will, someday soon."

He leaned forward to kiss her, but C.G. put a hand between them.

The swing stopped, and C.G. wasn't breathing. The natural woman in her wanted Drake's kiss. The rational woman knew it shouldn't happen.

She lowered her hand from his strong, firm mouth, down to his chest, where she felt the vibrant beating of his heart. And it matched her own.

"I want to kiss you, C.G.," Drake whispered, his eyes imploring her to forget her resolve and surrender to the delicious moment of his tenderness.

"I. . .I want it, too."

"Then let me—" He leaned toward her, but she backed away from him.

"Please don't tempt me."

He didn't smile, and she was glad. She didn't want his pursuit of her to be a game for him, a pleasant challenge to add zest to the tedious chore of merging two banks.

"Can I tempt you?"

"Of course. I'm not made of stone."

"No, you're not, but you're as exquisite as the finest marble statue of any Greek goddess."

C.G. laughed lightly. "I am not a goddess."

"You could be in my eyes."

She shook her head no. "You need to be seeing God."

"Maybe I see Him in you."

C.G. took a deep breath and let it out very slowly. Was she being a good witness for Jesus? Somehow she doubted it, for Drake didn't seem to understand what she was trying to say about priorities. "I wasn't playing hard-to-get earlier today, Drake," she said, "when I told you I don't want a relationship with a workaholic."

"You keep using that word, C.G., but it does not apply to me."

"No?"

"I love my work. I'm good at it. I work hard and long hours. What's wrong with that?"

"Nothing, as long as it doesn't make you give up more important things."

Drake stopped the swing and looked at her. "Who gave up

important things, C.G., and turned you against ambitious men?"

He'd thought she wouldn't tell him, but she did, and rapidly.

"My uncle is rarely home, hasn't taken a vacation for years, misses many special events that involve his wife and children. But he makes lots of money.

"Dottie's husband wants to be top cop, so he works double shifts, volunteers for extra duty, and isn't even aware that Dottie is on the verge of having an affair with his best friend.

"I had a fiancé who thought so much of marrying me, that he said on the night we were planning our honeymoon, 'You don't mind if I schedule a meeting with some associates in Miami, do you? An all-day meeting will really cement a number of tentative business relationships.' His ambition severed our relationship."

Drake looked seriously into her eyes. "I am not those men, C.G. When I marry, I'll give a hundred percent of myself to my wife and family, and I'll never miss my children's baseball games or vocal recitals."

Even as he said the words that sounded so right, Drake searched his heart and wondered if he would keep those promises. He was a man of ambition. A man who didn't really know how to put anything else before his work. C.G. was probably right to steer clear of him.

He started the swing moving again.

If he were smart he'd say, Okay, let's forget the whole thing. If he were smart. But something about C.G. made him think she had some insight into living that was escaping him at the present. Maybe he needed her more than he wanted her.

"Are you against the accumulation of wealth?" he asked her.

She gaped at him. "Absolutely not. I'm not naive or simple, Mr. Forrest. I fully intend to drive a Porsche myself, some day. In order to get that car, though, I'm not going to give up what's really important—a full relationship with Jesus Christ, a knowledge that I'm walking in His will and that I can call on Him at any time to guide me and give me His peace. What could be more wonderful than that?"

The phone rang, and Drake jumped up and was already at the

door when Gwen met him on the other side of it.

"That wasn't Henry," she told him. "Sorry."

He grunted. "Well, I can make this day productive while I'm waiting. Gwen, do you know the circuit identification numbers for the Blue Ridge branch?"

She wrinkled her forehead. "No, I don't. Why do you need them?"

"We're changing the analog data lines to digital, so in order to disconnect the proper circuit, I need its exact identification number. All the numbers will be on your network interface, probably in some equipment room where the circuits are terminated."

"We have a small room that's little more than a closet, where the phone company has installed all the circuits," Gwen told him. "It's nothing fancy. Just a piece of mounted plywood that has various jacks on it."

"That's what I need."

Gwen's eyes brightened. "Shall we go now?"

"Sure."

Drake turned to C.G. "Would you mind staying here, C.G., in case Henry calls or comes over?"

C.G. did most definitely mind playing babysitter to his sports car while he and Gwen spent time in a tiny closet at the bank, but she could hardly admit that.

"Of course I'll stay," she assured him.

"That's my girl," he said exuberantly, and Gwen's head snapped around nearly 180 degrees to stare at C.G.

fifteen

Drake went off to the bank with Gwen, and C.G. read a magazine and glanced every five minutes at the clock above the kitchen sink. If Henry didn't come sooner than expected, she was going to miss her six o'clock date with Jeffrey, and would have no way to get in touch with him. She would hate him thinking she had stood him up when she hadn't meant to.

Though her mind was filled with imaginings of what Drake and Gwen were doing at the bank, she just kept turning the pages of the magazine, seeing very little of what lay on them.

How can I be so attracted to someone who is the epitome of what I do not want in a man? she questioned herself. Ambition and success were admirable traits. She had them both herself, though to a much lesser degree than Drake Forrest.

He, however, was in the big leagues, and had given up his spiritual life to get there. Could he change? Learn to put his work after his family and relationship with God?

She had known of too many women who had married a man with a problem, sure he would change once he had a wife and family, only to have that dream shattered with the reality that people don't often change—unless they have a personal encounter with the God of the universe, and His Son, Jesus Christ.

The trouble was, Drake was already a Christian, 'though out of fellowship. He knew the Scriptures, knew the kind of life he should be leading, but had chosen another way instead. He was worshiping success at any cost rather than worshiping God who loved him and had died for him.

C.G. gripped the magazine to her breast and prayed for wisdom in her relationship with Drake. He was a determined man, and he wanted her. He would not give up his campaign to win her. How could she keep from falling in love with him and still be his friend?

When she heard a car door slam in the driveway an hour later, she raced to the window, hoping it was Henry. It wasn't. Drake and Gwen were back and walking toward the house.

C.G. took a deep breath to calm her racing heart and hoped her face wasn't flushed. She'd missed him. She'd missed Drake as though he were special to her, important, a person she wanted to be around, a lot.

"Hi," he called out to her with a grin when she opened the door and greeted them. He looked pleased, which had to mean he'd found what he was looking for or had enjoyed himself with Gwen.

C.G. chastised herself for thinking that. It was all Dottie's fault for putting the idea into her head that Drake Forrest was a womanizer. Here at the house, his behavior toward Gwen had been perfectly circumspect. Still, C.G. couldn't help wondering just how small that closet at the bank was.

Gwen's facial expression was a stark contrast to Drake's. While she was not out-and-out scowling, she was not a happy camper either.

Drake bounded up the porch steps and stopped in front of C.G., his eyes drinking her in.

"Miss me?" he asked. She knew he was teasing, maybe, and answered in kind, in her best Scarlett O'Hara imitation.

"I couldn't concentrate on a thing while you were gone. My poor head was just a muddle."

Drake laughed uproariously and turned to say something to Gwen, but she swept past them both and into the house before he got a word out, and allowed the screen door to bang closed behind her.

C.G. looked up at Drake. "What happened?"

His gaze became serious, along with the slant of his mouth. "Nothing, C.G. Absolutely nothing."

"I see." And she did, and she was glad. For some reason she wanted to know that Drake was smarter than to fall for Gwen's homespun designs on him. It seemed he had been loyal, too, to his declaration that he wanted C.G. to be the woman in his life.

"Has Henry called?" he asked, his eyes flitting back to his car.

"No. Sorry."

But just as the words were spoken, a beat-up, rattling, old, blue Ford 250 pickup truck groaned into the driveway. On its side was painted, probably in the 1940's, the identification *Henry's Garage*, and under it the words, *We do it right.*

Drake's relieved look turned to one of grave concern, and C.G. wondered if he would actually turn over his forty thousand dollar baby to this grizzled man of indeterminate age who groaned getting out of the truck, whose huge belly protruded from greasy suspendered pants, and who moved with all the speed of an ancient turtle.

"Hi y'all," he called out, and Drake hurried to meet him. "Didn't have to go to Atlanta after all," he explained his early arrival. "Friend of mine in Ellijay had just what you need."

"Great!" Drake exclaimed.

A few minutes later the 'Vette was up on a hydraulic jack and Drake was squatted beside Henry, sharing an animated conversation that had as its focus their mutual love affair with this particular make of automobile. One would think they'd known each other all their lives instead of just five minutes.

C.G. sat on the swing and admired the litheness of Drake's body as he stooped, or stood, or bent over. He was in great physical condition, moving with a fluidity that came from honed muscles and regular exercise. He certainly was one appealing combination of mind and body that she couldn't help but admire.

Then something happened that showed another side of him. A small boy, aged eight or nine, dirty, poorly clothed, and in bare feet, with bushy, unkempt hair, came shuffling down the sidewalk. He looked unhappy and his little shoulders heaved now and then, as if he'd been crying and was trying to stop but couldn't.

The sound of Drake and Henry talking caused him to look up, and C.G. almost laughed out loud at how big his eyes grew when he saw the gleaming black car, the likes of which, it was easy to guess, he'd never seen before.

He stopped where he was while his mouth slowly dropped

open. He became a statue, not moving, barely breathing, but his eyes darted back and forth from the car to Drake and back again to the 'Vette.

It was several minutes until Drake noticed him. Then he smiled and called out to him. "Do you want to see the car?"

The boy stood where he was, not moving an inch, just staring.

"It's all right," Drake assured him, taking a step toward him, which made the boy move backward defensively. "You can see it better close up." Drake stood quietly, not moving, but smiling, until the youngster slowly, cautiously, inched his way forward.

"It's a Corvette," Drake said, his hands locked behind his back.

When the boy was close enough to touch it, he did not do so, but put his hands behind his back, just like Drake, who then began a painstakingly slow walk around the magnificent machine. The boy imitated him, and C.G. held her hand over her mouth, wishing she had a camera with which to capture the moment.

"I can't let you get in until the car comes off the jack," Drake said, "but I'll take you for a ride later, if you'd like."

The boy gawked up at him, amazed at the invitation, as was C.G. who hadn't thought Drake would want so dirty a tyke in his immaculate automobile.

The boy stayed, squatting down beside Drake and watching the work in progress, just like the big man was doing while he talked with Henry. It was a Norman Rockwell slice of American life, three males united for a moment by a common love for a gorgeous hunk of metal.

Gwen came out of the house and joined C.G. on the swing. She seemed perkier and smiled as she whispered, "Henry's the best. He may not look like much, but there's no one within a hundred miles who knows more about cars than he does."

"That's good. Did everything go okay at the bank?"

"Yes, fine." Gwen turned and look straight at C.G. "Is there something going on between you and Drake Forrest?"

C.G.'s eyes widened in surprise. "No, Gwen, nothing."

"Mmm, you could have fooled me. He must have asked me a dozen questions about you."

"He's probably checking out my qualifications to stay on once the acquisition is completed. I was told by one of our vice presidents that not everyone will keep his job."

"Is that so? Oh, I hope I keep mine."

"I do, too, Gwen. You're good here. We can depend on you."

Gwen looked surprised with the compliment. "Thanks. I appreciate knowing that." She looked over at Drake and began to shake her head back and forth. "I don't think that's the reason he was asking questions about you," she said.

"You don't?"

"Nope, because he came right out and asked me why you're not married."

She got up and went back into the house, leaving C.G. stunned, and wanting to know what the other questions were. *So*, C.G. thought, *he isn't giving up on me after all, and doesn't care if others know of his intentions.*

The object of her thoughts jogged over to the porch and gave her a winsome smile. A lock of hair splayed over his forehead and there was grease on his fingers, but the radiant look in his eye told her he was having a glorious time.

"Henry says we'll be on our way in five minutes." He looked at his watch. "Add to that another ten or so. I'd like to take Danny for a ride, if you don't mind."

C.G. smiled warmly even while she thought of Jeffrey Brandon standing on her front porch in just a few hours, receiving no answer to his knock. "I wouldn't mind at all. He's thrilled with the attention you're giving him."

"He's a good kid. Bright. We'll still get back to Cheston by five-thirty," he promised, then gave her a mischievous grin and added, "even if I don't drive fast. I know that's later than either of us wanted, but at least we won't have to spend the night here." His expression grew serious. "Would you have minded?"

"It would have been awkward, don't you think?"

"No, I don't, because I would have had Gwen drive me to a

motel. There's one not far from the bank."

"Oh."

Drake didn't quite know what to make of C.G. Grady. On the one hand she was sophisticated, mature, and well educated, as evidenced by her position with the bank and her appearance which showed style and good taste. On the other hand, there were moments when he caught an innocence about her, as though she were on unfamiliar territory in being with a man.

Surely, at her age, she must have had one or two meaningful experiences with someone. Women didn't save themselves any more for the man they married. Not like his mother, and her mother before her had done. Times were different nowadays. Self-gratification was accepted as the norm. Self-restraint was unusual.

He knew any number of women who would have used such a situation as he and C.G. had faced, to foster a more intimate relationship with him. C.G., however, struck him as a woman who was not interested in that kind of liaison. She wanted more from a man. She deserved more.

He looked at her with new eyes, knowing more than ever that he wanted her in his life. For how long or how seriously, he wasn't sure, but he knew he had at least four months to win her over, and there was no doubt at all in his mind that he would do just that.

sixteen

Henry finished the 'Vette, and C.G. went out to meet Drake's newest friend, little Danny, and watched with pleasure when the boy's eyes grew huge and unbelieving as Drake made good on his invitation to take a ride in the fancy car.

The "ten-minute ride" that Drake had promised turned into fifteen and C.G.'s heart sank, knowing she could never get home and changed before Jeffrey came to take her to dinner.

They said good-bye to Gwen and thanked her for the lunch and snacks and other help, and when they went to get into the car, Drake surprised C.G. by suggesting she drive home.

"Are you kidding?" she asked. "You'd trust me with your baby?"

"I'd trust you with anything, C.G." His eyes softened. "Besides, you'll be more comfortable, won't you, behind the wheel? And less likely to throw up if you're not sailing from side to side around those four hundred curves between here and Cheston." He winked at her.

"Ah, I see. So your grand gesture is not altruistic after all?"

"I always take care of what's mine."

&

At exactly 5:32 p.m., they drove onto the winding, private, graveled road that led to C.G.'s house. It had been a dream driving the Corvette, and C.G. had thoroughly enjoyed doing so, with the top down, the wind whipping her hair.

Now, though, there were other things to do. Because of everything that had happened, she was going to have far too little time to get herself ready for her dinner date with Jeffrey.

She scrambled out of the car before Drake even had a grip on the door handle on his side and went to the front and waited for him and said, "I'm sorry the day was such a mess, but we did get what we went after, and now you can work tomorrow to your

92

heart's content. I guess I'll see you on Monday."

She turned and ran up the three steps to the porch, knowing she'd been babbling, hoping he hadn't picked up on her nervousness.

"Yes, it was a good day, C.G.," Drake agreed, and instead of leaving, he sauntered slowly across the front of her one-story country home, scanning the curtained windows, the three hanging baskets of geraniums along the front of the porch, the dried arrangement of magnolia blossoms fastened to the front door.

"This is really nice. Yours?"

"Mine and the bank's." C.G. got out her keys. Hopefully, he'd get the message.

He didn't.

"This porch is wide," he commented, stepping up on it, and going to one of two heavy, maple rocking chairs. He eased his long frame into it and gave a long and deep sigh. "I could sit here all night."

C.G.'s palms were moist.

"Do you use it a lot?" he asked, looking out across her finely mowed lawn, scattered here and there with groups of marigolds and zinnias.

"Yes. I like to read here." The key was in the door. She unlocked it. "Well, Drake, I must say good-bye." She watched him turn, a surprised expression on his face as he slowly rose to his feet.

"Am I being given the bum's rush?" he asked.

"Not at all," C.G. exclaimed, embarrassed, mentally ticking off exactly how long it would take her to shower, apply fresh makeup, and select an outfit to wear. She must have been unconvincing because Drake came up to her and said, "You have plans for this evening, don't you?"

"Well, yes, I do."

He looked at her long and hard. "You should have told me."

"Probably."

"Why didn't you?"

C.G. didn't know what to say. After all, it wasn't as though she were doing something wrong, that she were going out with someone else behind his back.

"It doesn't matter," she said, trying to sound offhanded, as though the whole situation was minor. "I'm here now, so—"

Drake's hands captured her shoulders and held her firmly. "Oh, but it does matter, C.G. Why didn't you tell me you were going out?"

"It wouldn't have made any difference. We couldn't have gotten the car fixed any sooner. True?"

Besides, what could she say that wouldn't sound ridiculous: I have this date, but it's not with someone I care about, at least I don't think I care about him, although maybe I could someday, but really I wish I were going out with you instead?

She hesitated too long because Drake's eyebrows raised, as though he had just figured something out.

"It's a man, isn't it?" Those same brows dipped in an ominous frown. "You're expecting him at any minute, and you don't want him finding me here." His hands tightened on her arms.

"I need time to get ready."

"You're gorgeous like you are."

Did he see her like that? Even after the long day? She couldn't have a shred of makeup on. Her hair had been blown to smithereens in the convertible.

C.G. wanted to look away from him, but couldn't. In his eyes, for the briefest of moments, she saw something she had not seen before in him: uncertainty, and it took her breath away. Drake Forrest knew his abilities, his power to make things happen. Here, with her, he was not in control, not able to make things happen the way he wanted them to.

"What's his name?" he asked, his tone knife sharp.

Hearing his question, asked as if he had every right to know what she did every moment of her life, caused C.G. to turn out of his grasp and reach for the door handle. But before she could open it, Drake's hand was on hers.

"Is he someone special, C.G.?"

Now she was irritated. What gave him the right to ask such a question? She stabbed him with a look as sharp as his previous words. "I really don't have time to discuss my love life, Drake."

"Love life?"

Drat. Poor choice of words. "I have to get ready."

"Fine. Go right ahead." Surprisingly, he released her, and his change of mood from interrogation to cooperation left her wary.

"Go ahead? No more personal none-of-your-business questions?"

"Nope." He spun on his heels and walked to one of the rockers and sat down.

Puzzled, C.G. followed him. "What are you doing? I thought you were leaving."

"Before meeting your date? Not on your life, sweetheart."

"I'm not your sweetheart, Drake Forrest, and I have not invited you to meet my date." C.G. glanced at her watch. Quarter to six. She'd never get ready in time.

"I'm inviting myself," Drake replied.

"Why?" She was getting exasperated.

The look of innocence he gave her was worth a thousand words. "To see if he's worthy of you."

"What?"

"Which, of course, I know right now that he isn't."

"Drake Forrest, get off my porch. Get off my property." C.G. plunked her hands on her hips and faced him with grit.

He just smiled and said softly, "Make me."

C.G. wanted to wring his neck. Of course, she'd have about as much chance to do that successfully as she would in physically evicting him from the premises. He was a big man, with at least a seventy-pound advantage over her, not to mention strong, powerful hands and a determination to match the most aggressive bulldog.

She turned abruptly and stormed to her front door, yanked it open, heard his soft chuckle, and slammed the door once she was inside.

The nerve of that scoundrel, she fumed, stomping into her bedroom, flinging open the closet door, seeing absolutely not one thing she could wear that night, then deciding on kelly green slacks and a matching long-sleeved blouse, neither of which fit her very well, but what difference did it make anyway? Drake was going to be there when Jeffrey arrived, and would ruin the evening before it even started.

She hurried through her shower, heard Drake whistling on the front porch, then heard the crunch on gravel as a car came up her driveway.

She peeked through the window and saw Jeffrey getting out of the car. *Oh no*, she groaned, standing there dripping wet. *I have to throw something on to go out and greet him before Drake sends him packing.*

But it was too late for that. The men were shaking hands. The men were talking. The men were sitting down in the rockers.

seventeen

Frantically C.G. dried herself off, dried her hair, got dressed, added gold earrings and some dangly bracelets to her outfit, which didn't look as bad as she'd thought it would as it defined her figure nicely without being suggestive.

Stepping out on the porch fifteen minutes later, the animated conversation Jeffrey and Drake were having about baseball abruptly ended. Both jumped to their feet as she walked toward them.

She had to admit it was a heady sensation to see pure, male admiration from both of them, but it was in Drake's eyes that she saw a devilish grin that made her want to kick his shins.

"I see you've met each other," she tried to say without malice in her voice.

"Yes." Jeffrey came over to her. "Drake tells me you're working together, and just had a rough day in Blue Ridge. He explained why you're running late."

"Did he?"

C.G. turned her eyes to Drake who nodded, innocence personified. She could only imagine what else he'd told Jeffrey, or what impression he'd given about their relationship.

"Well, folks, I have to be going," Drake said cheerfully. "It was nice meeting you, Jeffrey. Enjoy your dinner." He turned to C.G. who was thrown off guard by his intent to leave. She'd half believed he would ask to join them for the evening.

The two men shook hands, and Drake turned to C.G. "Could you walk me to the car, C.G.? I have something to tell you."

"About the acquisition?" she asked sweetly.

"Yes, of course."

"Excuse me, Jeffrey, I'll be right back," she told him.

At Drake's Corvette, he turned and gave her a winning smile. "Have a good time."

His accepting attitude made her suspicious. "Why do I think there's more to that good wish than a good wish?"

"There's nothing at all misleading in it. I hope you enjoy yourself. Jeffrey's a neat guy."

"You think so?" She was amazed. She'd half thought Drake would have driven him off. Hadn't he claimed her as his own, back at Smith's General Store? Was he giving up on her already? Of course, why shouldn't he, since she'd told him in no uncertain terms that she wasn't even looking for a man, much less a man like him.

"Did Jeffrey tell you he's a minister?"

"Sure did. Sounds like he has quite a church down in Florida."

"I haven't seen it, but from what he says, it's dynamic and growing."

"Lucky for those kids to have a man like him to guide them."

C.G. knew something was missing here, and she found out what it was in the next words out of Drake's mouth.

"The kids are lucky, like I said, but you realize, of course, that Jeffrey Brandon is not the man for you." The confident look on his face was maddening.

"You've decided that, have you?"

He nodded. "That's right. It's easy to see. Oh, he's a nice guy. Genuine. Committed."

"But?"

"Not the man for you."

"Well, thank you for informing me. I never would have figured it out for myself."

Drake fixed on her a look that could only be called that of a male caveman claiming his female. "I told you back at the General Store that you were mine. And I meant it. Jeffrey Brandon is no threat to me."

He climbed into the 'Vette while C.G. seethed.

He started the engine. "Oh, by the way, what time should I pick you up tomorrow?"

"Tomorrow?"

"Yes. I'm taking you to church."

"You're what?"

Drake laughed. "You know, Miss Grady, you ask a lot of questions. What time does the service start?"

"I go for Sunday school. Way too early for you."

"Not at all. What time?"

"I usually leave at nine o'clock, but I am not going with you."

"Why not?"

C.G. stepped closer to the car, to be sure Jeffrey couldn't hear her words. "This won't work, Drake, this sudden interest in going to church when I know you gave it up long ago. It's nothing more than a cheap attempt to get on my good side."

"You're wrong, C.G. You've made me see the light. The error of my ways—"

"Oh, please, stop. You can go to church every day for the next year and still not be the kind of Christian man I want, and need."

"I understand that, but this is, at least, a start."

"Then find any church you want, and go to it."

"I want to go to yours."

"Fine, but not with me."

"Why not with you?"

"Because I won't be manipulated." She leaned over and glared at him. "Do you think I'm that naive to believe your sudden change of heart is genuine?"

"Okay, but it will be on your conscience if I decide not to go tomorrow because I won't know anyone."

"Poor excuse for staying away."

"If I never find the way back. If my soul is lost forever—"

"All right, all right. Pick me up here at nine o'clock, but I warn you, Drake, if you're not sincere in this, you won't get as much as a smile out of me the rest of the time we work together."

"See you then." And he drove the Corvette slowly down the driveway while C.G. condemned herself for falling into what surely must be a honeycombed trap.

⁊

His mother's home-cooked meal of beef stew, slow cooked for sixteen hours in a crockpot, bakery-style blueberry muffins, and pumpkin pie for dessert, was his father's favorite. It was also Drake's.

After apologizing for being late, then eating more than he should have, he sat in his parents' living room and listened to what they'd been doing lately and felt contented in a way he knew he hadn't been for a long time.

His dad, a tall, virile man of sixty with a flat stomach and a full head of brown hair once red, a retired firefighter, sat in his favorite recliner and recounted what he was doing in the rose garden, and in his basement workshop. "That circular saw you got me for Christmas makes easy work of cutting landscape timbers," he told Drake.

"I'm glad you're using it, Dad."

Despite his father's recitation of activity, Drake noticed a decided lethargy about him. He hoped it was just routine tiredness.

"He always puts the tools you give him to good use," Katherine Forrest insisted.

She looked particularly pretty to Drake tonight, wearing a wide-legged, one-piece hostess outfit of black and lavender that emphasized her still slender waist. Her soft blond hair was newly-styled in a full, stacked cut that swept toward her cheeks, and her aqua eyes danced with love which Drake felt strongly every time she looked at him.

He, of course, was urged by his parents to tell about his life, and got a little lengthy in explaining the bank acquisition.

"Tell us more about this person you're working with at Ashford Bank and Trust," his mother urged.

Katherine Forrest had listened carefully to her son for nearly a half hour and had picked up on a pattern: no matter what subject Drake talked about, he invariably came back to this "person" he was working with to coordinate the acquisition. So far he had said she was nice, intelligent, capable, and had a sense of humor. It was what he had not said that worried her.

"Is she young?" Katherine asked.

"Younger than me."

"Pretty?"

"Very."

"Married?"

"Single."

Katherine took a long, slow breath. "Would you both excuse me for a minute."

As quickly as she could, she went to the farthest room in the house and called Jane Grady.

"We're going to have to step up our efforts," she told her matchmaking partner. "My son is interested in another woman."

"Oh, no."

"What's worse is that they'll be working together for months."

"Does it sound serious?" Jane asked.

"I'm reading between the lines at this point, Jane, but we need to do more than send our children written teasers. Is your Chryssie showing any interest in my son?"

Jane giggled. "So far she thinks he's a dog."

"A dog?" Katherine responded indignantly. "Jane!"

"It's not what you think. Chryssie got the wrong impression from my veiled teasers and thinks her father and I are getting her a Cocker Spaniel."

Katherine laughed. "She's going to be a bit surprised, don't you think, when she meets Drake."

"I'll correct that impression the next time I talk with her."

"You'd better make it soon. Tonight, if you can."

"I'll try. Do you think it's time to send a picture?"

Katherine thought a moment, then said, "I suppose, although I wish they could come to appreciate each other's sterling qualities first. Why are young people so hung up on good looks nowadays?"

"To tell the truth, Katherine, I think they were in our day, too."

"Perhaps you're right. Anyway, when we see each other at Bible study this week, let's exchange pictures. Small ones, of course. I think an 8x10 color would be too hard a sell, don't you?"

"Yes. See you on Tuesday."

eighteen

Back in the living room, Katherine went to a tall bookcase and pulled from one of the shelves several picture albums. Sitting down on the sofa, next to her son, she said, "Let's look these over, shall we? They bring back so many wonderful memories."

Drake loved looking at family pictures, even ones of him when he was younger and looked funny, in his own eyes.

"Look at this one, Mother." Drake pointed to the picture used for his high school yearbook.

"You look so young there, dear."

"That's because I was. Look how light my hair is. It's getting darker."

"That's what happens to blonds, I guess. Where's your graduation picture from college?"

They found it, and Drake was surprised at how much he had changed in the intervening years. His face was more defined now, cheeks narrower, his eyes more intense. He had a little less hair, too, but not by much.

His mother was now skimming rapidly through the pages. "What are you looking for?" he asked her.

"Don't we have a current picture of you? One that shows how devastatingly handsome you are?"

Drake laughed and his father guffawed, "Did we ever have one that showed that?"

"Yes, Kevin, we must have." Katherine was getting frustrated as she flipped over one page after another. "All these pictures, and not one I could give to—" She stopped abruptly.

"Give to whom, Mother?"

"Well. . .to anyone. . .who needs one. . ."

Drake threw his hand down on the photo album she was holding on her lap. "Don't tell me you're looking for a picture to show this mystery woman I'm supposed to fall in love with on your recommendation."

"Mystery woman?" his father questioned.

Drake turned to him. "Hasn't Mother told you she's been sending me little teasers of information about the daughter of some friend of hers she thinks is perfect for me?"

"Katherine, you never told me," Kevin Forrest blustered. "Who is this person?"

"She's Jane's daughter, Kevin. I'm sure I've mentioned her to you?"

"I don't remember you doing so."

"Oh, I must have." Katherine was flustered with two men staring at her as though she had just committed murder. She deliberately had not mentioned Chryssie Grady to Kevin because he would have been against the idea. Men never put any faith in matchmaking. But mothers did, and she wasn't giving up on getting Chryssie together with Drake.

Her son stood up abruptly, closed the book on her lap, scooped the other albums up in his arms and returned them to the proper shelf. "Enough of looking at pictures."

"Drake, you're being uncooperative."

He gave her a patient grin. "Yes, I am."

"But she's a lovely girl."

"Look, I appreciate your wanting to help my love life along, but I'm not interested."

"How can you say that when you've never met her?" Katherine questioned. "Weren't you at all intrigued with the information I sent you about her?"

"No."

"I don't believe it."

"Believe it, Mother. I want to do my own looking."

"You can't be everywhere at once. That's why God created mothers—to help."

Drake chuckled and came back to the sofa. Giving his mother a kiss on the cheek, he said nicely, "I know your heart is in the right place, but I want you to give up this matchmaking."

Katherine's lower lip jutted out in a pout that made both Drake and his father laugh. "I can't," she said.

"Why not?" Drake wanted to know.

"Because this girl is right for you. If you would just meet her—"

"No."

"Once?"

"I think I'll have another piece of pie. Dad, would you like one?"

"Sure."

"Mother?"

She shook her head no, still pouting.

Drake sprang to his feet and fled to the kitchen where he cut two big pieces of pie and began to pour himself a glass of ice cold milk.

He hoped he hadn't hurt his mother's feelings. She was a sweetheart, a wonderful woman who loved him unconditionally and thought she had his best interests at heart.

What she could never do, though, in a million years was pick out the right woman for him. Someone he could love and admire forever. Someone like C.G. Grady.

The glass filled up and milk ran over onto the kitchen counter, and Drake didn't even notice as he stared off into space. He was thinking of C.G. and of going to church with her the next day.

He only snapped back to reality when a flashbulb went off and he heard the automatic advance of a 35mm camera. Looking up, startled, he saw his mother, a smug grin on her face, holding the camera that had done the deed.

"Motherrrr," he yelled after her as she scurried from the room and milk ran off the edge of the counter and onto his shoes.

❧

Drake picked C.G. up at nine o'clock and took her to church. On the way they stopped at the house of a Mrs. Ingles, a shut-in who only got out rarely, because of severe arthritis. C.G. took her some homemade peanut butter cookies, Mrs. Ingles' favorite, and a small African violet.

"Our Helping Hands ministry cleans her house and brings her groceries," C.G. explained on the way. "On days when she feels well, one of us will take her shopping for whatever she needs."

"How many people are in your group?" he asked.

"A dozen or so. We have no set schedule with anyone, but attend to needs as they arise." Her eyes misted. "It's a very satisfying ministry."

"A depressing one."

"Oh, no, not at all. To wipe away tears, and ease anxiety, maybe bring a smile to someone who has little to smile about— what could be more rewarding in this life?"

Drake was more in love with C.G. than ever.

The newly-built church where C.G. attended was located on a rocky hill. One looked up to see its brick form and white steeple rising toward the sky, then looked around to see the eye-catching landscape of pansies and azalea bushes sitting in islands of dark pine straw. There was no grass yet, but there was a view, from the parking lot, of Lake Lanier in the distance.

Although the building was only one year old, the congregation had been in Cheston for decades. There were ninety or so families who worshiped together and shared each others' triumphs and burdens, and love was there.

Drake felt it when he was warmly welcomed in the singles' Sunday school class after being introduced by C.G. to those present. The teacher, Helen Douglas, an attractive brunette with shoulder-length hair, a lawyer in her forties, was friendly, funny, spiritually mature, and understanding of what it was like to be an adult single in a world of pairs.

Drake realized, as the group read Scripture and discussed it, that he was happy with much of his life, but lonely for someone to share it with.

He made only one comment during the class, about the problem of finding women to date who could hold a man's interest. "I've dated beautiful women. I've dated intelligent and successful women, but after a few months the relationship is still shallow."

"That's why taking our time is important in getting to know someone," the teacher said. "Rushing into too serious a relationship can lead to all kinds of problems. Take it slow. Don't let physical desires overshadow the more important goal of learning what a person is all about. Take it slow," she repeated. "We can't afford to damage our lives by recklessly pursuing a relationship that might not be good for us."

Drake glanced at C.G., and found her looking back at him. The shimmering blue of her eyes held in their depths the very same question he was debating himself: could they have something meaningful together if they took it slow? He'd never been a man to go slowly. He didn't like the word, or its connotation for inaction. He had a quick mind and a rare ability to make accurate decisions in a short time. He had a reputation for it.

Now, though, after listening to this wise Sunday school teacher, and reading Scripture that advocated patience and control, he was beginning to rethink his campaign to win C.G. He wasn't giving up. Not one bit. It might be wise, though, to slow down, and plan a different strategy.

Fast or slow, C.G. was going to be his.

nineteen

Drake took C.G. to lunch after church, then drove her home where they sat in his car for a few minutes and talked, just talked. He did not attempt to kiss her. He wanted to; oh, how he wanted to, but he knew C.G. suspected he had only gone to church to get on her good side. And she was right. His motive had been far from pure. He told her so.

"What I didn't expect," he went on, "was to feel a strange hunger for something I haven't had in my life for a very long time."

"It's the God-vacuum in our hearts that can't be filled with anything or anyone other than God Himself," she explained.

"I was so sure it wouldn't mean anything to me—being in church, hearing and singing the familiar hymns, listening to the choir." He shifted in the seat so he could look directly at C.G. "The singles class was great. Then your pastor threw me a curve, speaking, as he did, with great conviction on the subject 'For what will it profit a man if he gains the whole world, and loses his own soul?'*

"The logic and encouragement of his words were meant for me, C.G. They spoke to my heart. I'm a man who owns a lot of the world. I've struggled to get to the top and have made it. But have I lost something more important along the way?

"I'm not sure yet. I'm still trying to sort out things in my head. All I know is that I've thought for too many years that success is proven by material possessions. To get those rewards, I've done my share of underhanded things, lost friends, and even made enemies. I don't have a best friend because I don't have time for one. I don't have a wife and children because I concentrate on myself and my own needs and desires.

"C.G.," and he took her hand, "how long ago did the pastor decide to preach on that text which has gripped my conscience,

*Mark 8:36

a man who hasn't gone to church for ten years?

"Why was I chosen by Georgia National Bank to oversee the merging of the databases of the two banks?" He paused, drinking in every feature of C.G.'s face. "Why are you the person I have to work with?"

"Those are a lot of questions, Drake. Do you know any of the answers?"

"Not a one, so far, but I'm pretty sure God is leading me to something, step by step, and I'd better pay attention."

❧

A month later, C.G. sat in her office, trying to concentrate. On the corner of her desk were a dozen, pale yellow roses, sent to her by Drake. She couldn't take her eyes off them. The petals were fragrant, and delicate, and reminded her of the gentle touch of his hands when he'd presented them to her. She also saw the thorns.

"Daydreaming of Prince Charming again?" Her assistant, Dottie Westfall, breezed into the room and collapsed in the vinyl chair in front of C.G.'s desk. "Last week it was Godiva chocolates. The week before a hardcover book you've been wanting for weeks, tied with silver ribbon. Just as I was beginning to think there wasn't a romantic man left in the universe, along comes Drake Forrest, and sweeps you off your feet."

C.G. gave her a look of disdain. "I'm not swept off. . .yet. I'm taking my time in making up my mind."

Dottie laughed out loud. "Really? Have you looked at yourself in the mirror the past few weeks? You're dewey-eyed—"

"I'm not."

"Radiant."

"Well. . ."

"And distracted."

"Distracted?"

"That's what I call it when you break off conversation in the middle of a sentence to stare out into the lobby and ignore the person speaking to you, which has been me, more than once. C.G., my friend, you're dancing on the precipice."

"Of what?"

"Falling in love, if you haven't already." Dottie leaned forward, and folded her arms on the desk. "With Drake Forrest. Admit it."

C.G. clucked her tongue against her teeth. "That's ridiculous, Dottie. I haven't known him long enough."

Since that first Sunday, when Drake had gone to church with her just to win her affections, and admitted the same afterward, he'd gone every week, and Sunday evenings, and for midweek Bible study, too. He was not a man to take things slowly, he'd told her, and she knew that from watching him at work. She just prayed he wasn't rushing into a recommitment that would be short-lived.

As far as their relationship was going, he was wooing her, slowly, carefully, in exquisitely thoughtful ways meant to defuse her natural wariness of him and his intentions. She knew this; he did not deny it. The fact that he was honest with her about his plans to bring her into his life led her, strangely, to trust him, but still she would not give in wholly until she knew he really was a changed man.

"You're doing it again." Dottie's soft chuckle drew C.G. from her contemplation, and she had to smile at herself. Her thoughts were never far from the man who had strode tall and strong into her life, and planned to stay. At least for awhile.

"I give up," Dottie exclaimed, hoisting herself out of the chair. "I'm amazed you keep your job when your mind is so often elsewhere."

She left with a cheery good-bye, and C.G. didn't even know why she'd come to see her until she saw a file folder in front of her with information she'd asked Dottie for.

I'd better get a grip on myself, she thought. *What if one of the vice presidents sees me the way Dottie does?*

She rose and took the file to her credenza where she put it in a drawer after taking some papers out. The task completed, her eyes fell on the picture of her parents, the one Drake had been so interested in the first day he'd been there.

Poor Mom, she thought. Looking back over the past month, her mother had been acting strangely. First of all, there was the conversation they'd had the day after Drake had taken her to church, when she'd gone to her parents' home for dinner. While putting away the leftovers, her mother had said, "Chryssie, I must clear up a misunderstanding."

That's when she'd learned that the adorable Cocker Spaniel she'd been expecting as a gift from her parents was really a grown man whom she was expected to dutifully meet and fall in love with, then marry.

"He's highly intelligent, dependable, protective, successful—" her mother had recited previously given information.

"Don't forget the mischievous eyes."

"Oh, yes."

"Mom, how could you be trying to set me up with this stranger? You know how I feel about blind dates and matchmaking."

"Yes, I do, but this man is exceptional. One of a kind. When you meet him—"

"I don't want to meet him, Mom."

"You'll like him, I know. I'm going to send you a picture of him."

C.G. groaned, and decided not to be too hard on her mom, whose heart, after all, was in the right place because she wanted what she thought was best for C.G.

"How do you happen to know this man?" C.G. asked.

"He's the son of a good friend of mine."

"Have you met him?"

"No, Chryssie, but his mother has told me enough so that I'm sure he's just what you need."

"You make him sound like Pepto Bismol."

"Not at all. He's quite handsome, and successful, and—"

"Mom, is he a Christian?"

There was silence and C.G. was surprised. Her mother felt the same way she did about the importance of a man and a woman sharing a strong faith. "He grew up in the church, Chryssie, and just needs the love of a good woman to bring him back. His parents have been praying for just that for years. And you know what it says in Proverbs 22:6."

"Yes, 'Train up a child in the way he should go, and when he is old he will not depart from it.' Still, he doesn't sound right for me, Mom."

"Well, of course there are no guarantees, but I think once you meet him, and go out with him for awhile, you'll know whether he's right for you or not. And, you could be a powerful influence on him for good."

"Mom, there's another man in my life right now who may turn out to be important." Then she told her mother about Drake, not by name or physical description, but that they worked together, and were attracted to each other, and that he, too, was searching for a spiritual life. "Probably nothing will come of our friendship," C.G. told her mom, "but I don't think I can handle two men at the same time."

She hoped she hadn't hurt her mother's feelings. "Do you understand where I'm coming from, Mom?"

"Yes, of course. Now, Chryssie, do you have a good photo of yourself? Just a small one. I've looked everywhere and can't find any that show your true personality that I can send to him."

C.G.'s heart lurched. "Him?"

"Why, yes, dear, the man we've been talking about for ten minutes. I heard what you said about this other man, but until something permanent is decided with him, I think you should keep your options open, and my friend's son is worth consideration. So please look through your pictures and bring me something as soon as you can, otherwise I'll give his mother whatever I have. His mother is going to give me a picture of him, as well. That may make him more interesting to you."

C.G. didn't know whether to laugh or cry.

A week later, when an envelope arrived in the mail with the words "PHOTO—DO NOT BEND" on the cover, she was not even tempted to open it, so turned off was she to the idea of two mothers scrambling to get their children together.

She put the photo envelope on a pile of newspapers in the kitchen, afraid to throw it out, but not planning to look at it in the near future either.

Then she lost it. Inadvertently tossed out with the papers, she guessed, and felt appropriately guilty, knowing all the trouble her mother had gone to to get this picture to her. What was she going to say when asked what she thought of him, this mystery man? She knew she could not lie to her mother, and dreaded the conversation to come.

twenty

It came four days later, when she met her mom after work to do some shopping together.

"Well, what did you think of his picture?" Jane Grady asked, as eager as a teenager over her manipulations. "Isn't he handsome? Doesn't his face show what a strong, dependable man he is?"

"Mom. . .I—"

"My friend said it wasn't the best picture of him. He was distracted when she took it."

"Mom. . .please—"

"She's going to try to get another one, but I guess he's stubborn. Doesn't want to meet you."

C.G. gasped with relief. "There you go, Mom. He doesn't want to meet me. I don't want to meet him. That should be the end of it."

Jane Grady looked at C.G. as though she had just materialized from outer space. "The end of it?" she cried. Then she shook her head. "The end of it will come only after the two of you sit down and get to know one other. Then, if you really find there is no common ground upon which to build a lasting friendship—"

"Motherrrr—"

"Then, and then only, will it be over." Jane stood to her feet, her facial muscles taut. She was not happy with her daughter's attitude. C.G. knew the look well. "You may pay for lunch," her mother announced, and left the restaurant ahead of C.G. and said precious little all the way to her home.

Before leaving the car, Jane asked, "By the way, you haven't told me what you thought of the man's picture." She turned in the seat of C.G.'s Mercury Cougar and waited.

C.G. cleared her throat and admitted softly, "I lost it."

She was not surprised when her mother got out of the car without saying a word. C.G. rolled down the window and called after her, "I didn't mean to."

She received no reply.

ঝ

Being a forgiving person, her mother called her in a few days, as cheerful as ever. No mention was made of the episode, and neither did she ask for a picture of C.G.

Sitting at her desk, now, at the bank, C.G. felt guilty because she had not sent her a picture. She knew she was being unusually stubborn about this matchmaking. Would it be so horrible for her to go along with the plan?

What could be the worst thing to happen? She wouldn't be forced to marry this stranger at gunpoint. All she had to do was meet him once, then tell her mother there was no way in a year of frozen Mondays that she wanted to see him again. There. Simple.

One thing she knew, this man, whoever he was, could not be better-looking than Drake. Or as smart. Or as successful. Or as attentive. Or as much fun to be with.

"C.G.? C.G.?"

She finally heard the voice of her assistant, James Wyatt, and she knew she'd been daydreaming, just like Dottie had said.

"Yes, James, what can I do for you?"

He was looking at her strangely, and beside him was a dowdy-looking woman who just had to be his mother. They had the same scowl, the same small mouth, the same straight nose that looked too short for the long face.

"C.G. I want you to meet my mother, Hilda Wyatt. Mom, this is C.G. Grady. We work together."

"She's your boss, don't you mean?" Mrs. Wyatt leaned forward and squinted as she looked C.G. up and down. "She's young, but not as pretty as you said."

Now it was James who was embarrassed.

"Mom's visiting me for awhile," he explained, "from Iowa, and wanted to see where I worked."

"How nice. How long will you be here, Mrs. Wyatt?"

"Until I decide to go home," came the curt reply.

She began walking around C.G.'s office, inspecting everything closely. "Why is her office so big and yours is so small?" she addressed James, and not C.G.

"I'm Miss Grady's assistant," James told his mother.

"Does that mean you have to have such a dingy, tiny office?" She glared at C.G.

"James is a valuable worker here at the bank," C.G. said. "I couldn't get along without him."

"Why don't you give him a bigger office, then? And a raise? He earns next to nothing."

Poor James. C.G. felt sorry for him. An indefinite stay from his mother was not going to be easy for him.

"Come on, Mother. I'll show you the rest of the bank." He turned to C.G. "Thanks for meeting her." He already looked exhausted.

"It was my pleasure." She turned to shake hands with Mrs. Wyatt and say something else, but the woman was toddling out the door, and as she did, she ran one finger over the top of the credenza, found just enough dust to have made the gesture worthwhile, and gave a little grunt of satisfaction as she moved into the lobby.

&

C.G. began to think Dottie was right about her being in love with Drake. He had been out of town for over a week, visiting the other bank branches, getting pertinent information, as he had in Blue Ridge, and C.G. couldn't believe how much she missed him.

At work, knowing he wasn't in his office, she felt a strange emptiness.

At noon, eating alone, she thought of the times Drake had taken her out for lunch, or had ordered in salads or pizza, or had brought in something he'd made himself, like the Italian meat loaf that was scrumptious. She'd been surprised he could cook, having thought he was always too busy to take the time to do it.

She had relented in her determination to remain aloof from

him when she'd learned from her Sunday school teacher that he was counseling with the pastor. "I don't know what it's about, of course," Helen had said, "but he must be serious about getting back into fellowship."

C.G. wanted to believe that, wanted to know he was sincere in his spiritual search.

It would be one thing for him to go to church with her; anyone could do that without really caring. But to talk with the pastor, well, there had to be something substantive about their conversations.

Drake came back on a Wednesday. C.G. saw him in the lobby and stood up and moved out from behind her desk, but dared not go further, for she knew she wanted to fly into his arms.

Susie Black called to him from behind her teller's window, but he only gave her a wave of the hand in greeting. His eyes were on C.G. all the time long, powerful strides carried him the distance to her office where he closed the door behind him and wrapped her in a look of pure adulation.

"I've missed you, Miss Grady."

"I've missed you, too."

"Do you know how much I want to take you in my arms? Right now? Kiss you? And I wouldn't care that the whole bank sees us."

C.G. nodded nervously, knowing she wanted him to do exactly that. They couldn't, of course, because they were at work where decorum had to be maintained, but his eyes, feasting on her, and the rigid way he stood, barely controlling his urge to do just what he'd said, let C.G. know how strong his feelings for her were.

"I'm glad you're back."

He took a step toward her. "I'm not sure how good my work was; my mind was distracted."

She reached down and took one of his roses from its vase and held it to her nostrils. "Thank you for these. I love roses."

"I love you."

He crossed the rest of the room and cradled her face in his hands, leaning over her, lowering his head until he kissed her.

The rose C.G. was holding fell to the floor as she released it to clutch his arms. "Oh, Drake, I love you, too," she said when he separated from her.

Over his shoulder she saw several of the tellers, including Susie Black, staring at them in amazement.

Her heart tumbled about in its cavity, its rhythm erratic as she tried to cope with Drake's saying he loved her, and her pledging the same.

"We've known each other such a short time," she said, stepping back from him before she did something impulsive, like throw her arms around his neck and kiss him ardently.

"Yes, but you're not like any woman I've ever known."

She felt a stab of insecurity, knowing there had been other women in his life. Had he told any of them he loved them? Was his telling her now just a line to get what he wanted?

With legs none-too-steady, C.G. leaned against her desk and said, "I think we should talk about this somewhere else."

Drake smiled. "Good idea. Then I can convince you of my feelings."

C.G. felt a rush of joy as well as one of caution. She wanted to ask him about his counseling with the pastor, wanted reassurance that he was serious about his coming back to the Lord and wasn't just playing a game to win her for a season.

He saw the concern in her eyes and brushed her cheek with the back of two fingers. "Don't worry, love." An eagerness exploded over his features. "I have tickets for the Gospel Singers concert tonight at the community center. Will you go with me?"

"Yes. I wanted to hear them. They're fantastic. When did you get the tickets?"

"The first night I went to see the pastor."

"The pastor?"

He smiled and daringly kissed the end of her nose. "I'll tell you about it later."

twenty-one

The concert was inspiring, thrilling, and even fun as the various musical numbers dealt with the joy of being a child of God, as well as the pain of being separated from Him.

It was unlikely that any person in the sold-out auditorium was not moved toward a deeper walk with the Lord. C.G. hoped that Drake was, too.

"There's a place I want you to see," he told her after the concert, and he took her to his apartment, on the fifth floor of a sophisticated complex in a prestigious area of north Atlanta.

Walking through the various rooms, C.G. saw the rugged individualism of Drake's personality carried out in the furnishings and accessories with which he surrounded himself. She could see him sprawled on the formidable bone-leather sofa and matching loveseat in the Great Room, pacing over the elegant forest green carpet that extended from room to room throughout the entire apartment, turning on the tall brass lamps, polishing the marble, almost life-sized horse's head on the wood and brass coffee table, explaining the detailed mountain mural over the fireplace that stretched fifteen feet, and nurturing the bonsai forest of pine trees on the mantel.

None of the furnishings crowded the rooms, but rather left ample space to move around and through, even in Drake's den, where a cherry wood home theater system took up one entire wall, and some bookcases covered two others.

C.G. examined the hardcover books there, which were mostly non-fiction, biographies, history, and mysteries, and was surprised to find a whole section of Christian and religious books, too, ranging through the centuries from Josephus to Luther, John Wesley to C.S. Lewis. Swindoll, Schuller, Dobson, Graham, and Peale stood with the others.

She turned to Drake. "You can't have read all these,"

she questioned.

He chuckled. "Not hardly. I just got them. But I'm making a dent. I've read three a week so far."

"Three? You must be a fast reader."

"Yes, fast."

As opposed to slow, C.G. thought, *which is what we are supposed to be doing in getting to know each other.*

On a round, cherry wood table beside a high-backed upholstered chair, C.G. saw a burgundy leather volume of Oswald Chambers' classic book, *My Utmost For His Highest.* On its cover, imprinted in gold, was Drake's name.

She sat down in the chair and picked up the book, admiring its feel, the smell of genuine leather, the fragility of the gilt-edged pages. "I've always wanted this book," she said. "My parents have a copy and I read it once years ago but have wanted one of my own."

With a smile, Drake went to one of the doors of the entertainment center, opened it, and brought out a small package wrapped in burgundy paper, tied with a gold ribbon. He handed it to her and sat down on a loveseat on the other side of the table to watch her.

"What's this?" she asked, but knowing from its feel that it was a book. Her eyes widened and she stared at him. "It's not . . .It couldn't be. . ."

Carefully, she slid the ribbon off the package and opened the paper without ripping it. Inside was a matching copy of Chambers' book, in burgundy leather, only with her own name imprinted in gold on the cover.

She gasped, "Oh, Drake, it's beautiful. And precious." She gazed deeply into his eyes which were filled with delight because she was so happy. "I'll treasure it, and read it every day."

Where a slender, burgundy ribbon marked a spot, she opened it and read the day's heading, "Spontaneous Love," and the Scripture portion from I Corinthians 13.

Her eyes filled with tears. How thoughtful he was. This, coupled with his diligent study of faith in the books he'd bought for his library, left C.G. with little doubt that he was a changed man. But would it last?

She leaned toward him, as he did toward her, and they kissed, sweet and lingering. "Thank you, Drake."

"I know the book will bless you, C.G. It already has me."

He told her then about his meetings with Pastor Horton.

"He's great, isn't he?" she said. "Down to earth? Understanding?"

"Agreed. Our talks together became a one-on-one discipling course. He figured me out pretty quick, that I was a materialistic guy who wanted to succeed more than anything."

"Which you've done."

"Yes, but at what price? Without going into a sermon, I know there's nothing wrong with being successful, but I gave up important things to be so."

From a Source not his own, Drake found the words to explain. "No more. God is now first in my life, C.G., and will remain so. I want to be in His service. I want to know I'm walking where He wants me to walk."

She clapped her hands like a child. "I'm thrilled for you, Drake. There's nothing in this world more satisfying than being right with God. There's unbelievable happiness, hope, contentment. . .oh, now you're a whole man. You're complete, in Him."

He smiled, then became serious. "I want you to know, C.G., that my relationship with God is not tied with you. If you walk away from me right now, and I never see you again, I still want to grow and stay in the center of God's will."

C.G. moved over to the loveseat and put her arm through his and laid her head on his shoulder. "I pray that will always be your commitment, Drake."

They sat there, quietly enjoying the closeness of the moment, until Drake said, "You think my decision was a hasty one, don't you?"

C.G. sat up, her expression thoughtful. "You must admit, Drake, that it happened quickly. You go to church with me one Sunday, and boom, there you are, a dedicated Christian again."

"It wasn't quite that fast, but yes, it does sound as though I did it, or pretended to do it, just to win you over."

"I don't want to think that."

"You don't have to." He placed his hands on her upper arms and held her away from him so he could focus on her questioning blue eyes that made him giddy inside.

"C.G., I've always been a decisive man. I make my living by rational and logical thinking. While there can be deep emotion in being a Christian, for me, after listening to the Sunday school lesson, and the pastor's sermon, then talking with him, it was a logical and rational decision to turn my life over to God. Completely. There weren't tears or fireworks for me, but I know it's real."

C.G. smiled. "'Come now, and let us reason together, says the Lord.'"

"Isaiah 1:18. I learned that one as a kid, but it was meant for me. I'm a reasoning kind of guy."

"Yes, you are, and what you're saying makes sense."

He stood up and she did, too. "It's getting late," he said. "Do you want to see the rest of the apartment or go home?"

"I want to see everything the fifty-cent tour allows me to see."

"You got it, lady," and he went to the impressive entertainment center and turned on his CD player. Soft, classical music floated through the whole house as they resumed a leisurely exploration.

A half hour later, they were sitting at the oval table in his cheerful breakfast nook, sipping glasses of sweetened iced tea, and Drake knew she belonged there. Her presence had left an image he would remember and feel long after she was gone—her moving through each room of his apartment, standing near this window, sitting in this chair, touching his books, complimenting his taste.

Before C.G. there had been a few friends, though not close ones, a few women, though not meaningful ones, places to go, things to do, but nothing that mattered much. He was a man consumed with the joy his work brought him, and when he got home, he wanted to relax, more likely than not by reading the latest technical journal in his field.

Thinking back on his rather lone-wolf existence, he supposed that was the price to be paid for becoming the best in his field, and he was the best, he knew.

But now what? With a thriving career, plenty of money, and a fine place to live, where was the next challenge? What things did he still need?

He had learned in the past weeks that things didn't speak to him in that golden voice of C.G.'s. Things didn't look at him with admiration and feel soft the way her lips did beneath his.

He and Pastor Horton had spoken of *things*, and how there's nothing wrong with acquiring them, as long as they don't take priority over a relationship with God.

He reached over and took C.G.'s hand and gently pressed the back of it to his lips. "Sweetheart, look at me." She did, and his heart warmed to the vibrant attention she gave him, her eyes shimmering blue pools under the glow of the polished brass chandelier above the table.

He was scared. More than scared, he was petrified that she'd say no. Turn him down. Never speak to him again.

For the first time in his adult life, Drake Forrest thought he might fail.

"C.G.," he began, then stopped.

"Yes?" The porcelain ivory of her forehead raised in question, and he longed to smooth it with his fingers.

Drake took a deep breath. *Here we go, Lord. Help me, will You?* With a tremor in his voice that reminded him of his high school days, he said, while squeezing her hand, "C.G., I love you. Will you marry me?"

twenty-two

C.G.'s eyes became giant saucers of surprise, then puzzlement, and she said nothing, but only stared at him. He felt the moments as an eternity.

"C.G.? What are you thinking?"

She swallowed. "I don't know what to say."

"Yes would be simple."

"I. . .I can't say that, Drake."

"Why? Because you don't trust me?"

"I'm sure you're sincere."

"Now. But only time will prove how deep my commitment is, right?"

"Yes."

"You told me you love me."

"I do, but. . ."

"What?"

"It's too soon to make so major a commitment. We've known each other such a short time, and even though you're counseling with Pastor Horton, and have made a recommitment. . ."

She paused, and he knew she didn't want to express her doubts out loud, but he knew what they were.

"You still wonder if my sudden return to church may be just to win you. Isn't that right?"

"No, no, not at all. I believe you when you say you've turned your life back to the Lord and. . .and I'm thrilled that you want to marry me."

Her hands were cold, and trembling, and he wanted desperately to make them warm and calm again.

"But we need time, to be sure of our love."

Drake caressed her hands then kissed the palms of both. "I will wait for you forever." His words were barely audible, but he knew she'd heard them when she reached up to a shock of his hair that had fallen across his forehead and gently, with her fingers, blended it back in place. Her touch made him shiver, gave him life, and hope, and he knew he would do whatever it took to make her his.

He leaned forward then, and with one hand raised her face to meet his kiss which was tentative at first, as though he had no right to be doing it, but when she did not pull away, but leaned into the kiss, he groaned and moved closer.

His hands felt the silken skin of her face; he smelled the delicious scent of perfume that she wore. It reminded him of honeysuckle—sweet, intoxicating, filling the air with dreams, and he stood and pulled her into his arms in a fierce embrace and deepened the kiss that was not like any he had ever experienced before.

She was his. She loved him.

They separated and opened their eyes at the same time and C.G. knew, with her heart, she was where she wanted to be: with Drake, in his arms, in his life.

Her rational mind, though, cautioned her to wait, to be sure.

"I'd like for you to talk with Pastor Horton," Drake said. "Get his impression of me, and my intentions."

She gave him a tender smile. "I'd rather make up my own mind, sir." She broke from him and went into the Great Room to retrieve her purse.

"I take it your answer is no to my proposal?" he asked.

"For now."

"So I should let the preacher go home, the one I've hidden in the laundry room all night who was going to marry us?"

"Most definitely." C.G. laughed, and the sweet sound of her voice only reinforced Drake's fascination with her. He really would have married her right then if her answer had been yes. It wasn't easy for him to wait, but he would, because he understood her hesitation and respected her wishes. She was wise and good, a lethal combination that made him love her all the more.

"I'd better get you home," he said. "As it is, we're both probably going to fall asleep at work tomorrow."

As he escorted C.G. toward the front door, he saw on the polished wood table in the foyer a stack of mail, and the envelope on top was in the familiar hand of his mother. He knew the big, red letters PHOTO, DO NOT BEND sprawled along one edge meant there was a picture inside of "the perfect woman" she wanted him to meet.

With a chuckle of patience toward his mother who never let go of a good project once she got started on it, he picked up the envelope, excused himself from C.G., strode into the kitchen where he tore it into four pieces—without opening it and looking at the picture inside—and dropped it into his trash compactor. Turning the knob to the right, with satisfaction he heard the grinding of the arm as it lowered to crush the envelope and its contents among the garbage and other trash.

"I don't need your matchmaking, Mother," he said softly. "I've found the perfect woman for me. All by myself."

He went to join C.G.

⬧

"What have you done to that man?" Dottie asked C.G. a week after the memorable night when Drake told her he loved her and asked her to marry him.

"What man are you referring to?" C.G. asked innocently, keeping her head down as she calculated a long row of complicated figures involving a comparison of voice and data communications for all twelve branches of Ashford Bank and Trust.

Dottie plunked down in the seat in front of C.G.'s desk and clucked her tongue. "I'm talking about that gorgeous male Drake Forrest who is trying his best to act as though you're nothing more to him than wallpaper, only he can't keep the glaze out of his eyes when he looks at you, or the longing from his voice."

"Oh, that man." C.G. peered up at Dottie. "Is he acting strangely?"

Dottie shook her head back and forth in disbelief. "Do you two really think you're fooling anyone? Well, I take that back. Susie Black is so dense she still thinks she has a chance with Drake. Have you noticed how she falls all over herself trying to do things for him?"

C.G. grimaced. "Yes, I have noticed."

"So, great boss, tell me all the details of your torrid romance."

"I can't tell you anything, Dottie. Not yet. Maybe someday."

Dottie squinted her eyes. "Ooo, that sounds serious."

"Could be, but we have to maintain a proper professional relationship here at the bank."

"I understand. Has he told you he's madly in love with you?"

C.G. looked over Dottie's shoulder and said nothing.

"Does he want to sweep you up in his arms and take you away from all this?" She waved her arm in a grand arc.

When C.G. still said nothing, Dottie grunted, "Okay, okay, I get the idea, but I want to be the first to know. . .when there is something to know."

Dottie walked out of the office just as Drake came in. "Hi there," she said to him, giving him a look C.G. was sure he would recognize as awareness of "the situation."

"Dottie," he responded with a smile, though he was looking at C.G. with large blue eyes filled with the same yearning she was feeling for him.

"Miss Grady, is that comparison of voice and data communications ready for me?" He stopped a respectable distance in front of her desk.

"Almost, Mr. Forrest. I'll have it on your desk in a half hour."

"Good."

Trying not to smile, he said, "I'll pick you up for the theatre right after work. *The Sound of Music* is one of my favorite plays."

"Mine, too."

"We'll have dinner first, in Atlanta, at The Plantation House. It's new, and they say the atmosphere takes you back a hundred and fifty years."

"I've never been there. It sounds. . .wonderful." The words came from deep in her throat and Drake reacted to them and took a step toward her, but then stopped when James Wyatt shuffled into the office.

"Oh, Mr. Forrest. Here are the figures you wanted." He handed a large manila folder to Drake and C.G. wondered what was in it. Drake hadn't told her James was working on a special project for him. She didn't like not being included.

"Thanks, James. You do good work," Drake said.

Has he done other things for Drake? C.G. wondered, staring at a thrilled James who was preening from the compliment, his shoulders thrown back, his chin raised.

Drake gave him his full attention. "How long have you worked here, James?"

"Three years."

"Plan to stay forever?"

James gulped. "I don't know. I guess that depends on what opens up, or if I have a good offer somewhere else."

Drake smiled. "It's good to have a career plan. Know where you want to be in five years. Ten years."

"Yes, sir. I have some ideas on that."

"I'd like to hear them."

Drake turned to C.G. "I'll expect that report on my desk, then, in a half hour."

"It will be there," she said, *along with a few questions*, she wanted to add. Since when had James and Drake become buddy buddy? It almost sounded as though Drake had some job in mind for James. What could it be?

When Drake left, she and James talked over some business and then she asked him what he'd given Drake.

"Just a comparison of voice and data communications for the past year."

C.G. frowned. That's exactly what Drake was waiting for from her. Why would he ask James for the same figures unless he didn't think he could trust hers?

C.G. felt a nagging concern over what was happening, and planned to ask Drake about it as soon as she took the report to his office.

A half hour later, armed with the statistics he'd requested, C.G. went to his secluded office to give them to him. He wasn't there, so she sat down and waited ten minutes, then left because she had an appointment with one of the vice presidents. She placed the folder with the information in the center of his desk and was frustrated because she hadn't been able to ask him about James.

twenty-three

"C.G., why haven't I received that report from you?"

It was Drake asking the question as she poured herself some coffee from the hospitality area in the bank's lobby. The stern expression on his face told her he was not happy with her.

"I left the folder on your desk more than an hour ago," she explained with a forced smile. She hadn't cared for his tone of voice and hoped no one else had heard him. Being reprimanded in public was not what professional colleagues did to one another.

"On my desk?" he questioned.

"Yes."

"Well, it's not there now."

C.G. frowned. "Maybe you moved it without realizing what it was."

"I don't think so."

"Why don't we go and look?"

Without waiting for his approval, C.G. moved quickly across the lobby and down the hall to Drake's office. Together they scanned his desk, and the other furniture in the room, but the folder was not there.

"I don't understand what happened to it," C.G. exclaimed. "I put it right here." She tapped the center of Drake's desk. "You were gone, so I waited a few minutes, then had to get to a meeting with Mr. Cole—"

"C.G., I need that report." His words were sharp.

She slowly crossed her arms over her chest and said, "Really? Didn't you get the same figures from James Wyatt? Why must you have them from me, too? Actually," she went on before he could answer, "I'm puzzled why you would ask the same report of both of us."

"Now don't get miffed, C.G.," Drake said, coming up to her and taking both her hands in his. "This is the way I do things.

With any important information, I get it from at least two sources, sometimes even three. You wouldn't believe how many errors creep into vital statistics. Yes, it's extra work originally, but in the long run it cuts costs and saves valuable time."

The logic of his procedure was not lost on her, but C.G. still felt he should have come to her, as division manager, and told her what he was doing.

"I'm sorry if you feel I overstepped your authority."

"I do feel that, but understand your method."

He gave her a lopsided grin. "Good. Shall we kiss and make up?" He put his arms around her waist and gave her a quick peck, but it still sent shivers to her toes.

They had just broken their embrace when James Wyatt appeared behind them.

"C.G., I picked up this folder by accident earlier when I came to see Mr. Forrest. I'd put some of my own work down on the desk while I waited for him to come back, and when he didn't, I grabbed up what I thought was mine, but it included yours as well."

He held the folder out to her, and C.G. flipped it open, checked its contents, then handed it to Drake. "I believe this is what you wanted."

He took it with a straight face, although she saw the regret in his eyes. "Thank you, Miss Grady."

James left and as soon as he was gone, Drake moved toward C.G. "Now where were we?"

C.G. scooted toward the door. "I'm out of here. Some of us have work to do and can't stand around being kissed and held in arms."

She hurried back to her office and quickly sat down, for her legs were weak. Another minute in Drake Forrest's arms and she would not even have noticed if the president of the bank had walked in and discovered them together.

❧

Something was wrong, very wrong. While her personal relationship with Drake was deepening each time they were together, their business relationship was changing, subtly. And C.G. didn't know why.

Looking back over the past three weeks, strange things had happened. Mysterious things she could not explain, but which had all pointed to her as being inept in managing the Information Systems Division.

It had started with the comparison of voice and data communications that Drake had asked for from both her and James. Incredibly, James' figures had been correct, while Drake had found several glaring, sloppy errors in hers. The matter was made worse because it proved to be an inaccurate transfer of numbers, so silly a mistake a first-year employee would not have made it. But it looked as though she had.

She was sure she hadn't, of course, but she also couldn't explain it.

Maybe Dottie was right in saying she was distracted thinking of Drake. It was getting harder every day at the bank to pretend he was only someone she worked with, and not the man she loved.

Oh yes, she loved him, completely.

Seeing Drake, hearing his voice, working side by side with him, without reaching over and touching his hand, or his face, or running her fingers through his hair, was far more difficult than she'd thought it would be when she'd insisted the night he proclaimed his love for her and asked her to marry him that they wait before making a permanent commitment to each other.

They were already committed, more and more, every moment they spent together. Drake was a wonderful man. A solid, dependable man who solved complicated problems at work easily, and just as easily fixed the leaky faucet in her kitchen sink. He mowed grass and painted fences and didn't mind strolling through a shopping mall.

They read together, current books as well as the Scriptures, and they had long discussions over doctrinal issues and how to live a Christ-centered life. His insight into the human character was amazing, and C.G. knew he was allowing God to bring him wisdom.

So, it was no wonder she had trouble concentrating on anything other than him. She remembered Dottie saying, "I'm amazed you keep your job when your mind is so often elsewhere."

Then there was the important meeting Drake called which was to be attended by her, Dottie, and James, to present them with a Proposed Implementation Plan. She was a half hour late, and Drake was livid. Controlled livid, because he was a professional, but livid nonetheless.

"It's nice of you to join us, Miss Grady," he ground out the words. "The three of us have gotten better acquainted waiting for you."

C.G. was puzzled. "I've been in a meeting with four other division managers until just now. According to my calendar, we were to meet at eleven o'clock," she looked at her watch, "which it is now—exactly. What's the problem?"

"The problem is that our meeting was scheduled for ten-thirty." Fiery dark eyes met hers and condemned her. In Drake Forrest's time frame, there was no excuse for lateness or misunderstanding.

C.G. distinctly remembered seeing the time on her calendar that morning before she'd gone to her other meeting. She was not about to blame her secretary for putting down the wrong time, which must be the explanation.

"I'm here now," she said, with a little smile which was not returned by Drake, though both Dottie and James looked sorry for her. "Shall we proceed?"

C.G. didn't really understand why Dottie and James were there anyway. Drake could have given her the information, and she could have passed it on to them on a need-to-know basis. For some reason, he wanted all three of them informed of what was going on. Was this another indication that he didn't trust her capabilities?

"As you know," Drake told them, "the acquisition date for Georgia National to take over Ashford Bank and Trust is set for December 15. Implementation of the merging of the data bases of both banks will be December 1. We'll switch to digital here, at the main branch first, but leave the analog service in place so the other branches can still communicate until we convert all the branches to digital, one branch a day."

He handed them a ten-page document entitled "Proposed

Implementation Plan" which listed the date the new system would be installed in each branch, the name and number of the equipment vendor doing the work, the name of each branch manager and phone numbers to that bank, contacts for the three telephone companies being used in the particular region each serviced, and the names and numbers of assistants in his office and his secretary should he need to be contacted. The document gave November 15 as the date when a Final Implementation Plan would be on C.G.'s desk.

"That does it." Abruptly, Drake stood and ended the meeting.

Dottie and James made a hasty retreat, but C.G. stayed, knowing she had to apologize even though she still did not understand the mixup, and wasn't happy with the fact that Drake was so upset by it.

Drake wanted to forget that C.G. had been late, but he couldn't. He was beginning to worry about her reliability. In the beginning, her work had been excellent and her cooperation and quick facilitating of needed information had made his job easier. But lately, inconsistencies were occurring that neither he nor she could explain.

Soon his contact at Georgia National Bank was going to ask if C.G. and her assistants should remain in their positions when the acquisition was completed. A month ago Drake would have given an immediate yes to all three. Today, he was reconsidering C.G., and he was in pain.

He loved this woman with his whole heart. He knew she was intelligent, capable, witty, lovable—his mind quickly turned from her business acumen to her adorable personality.

It had been the hardest thing he'd ever done, to work closely with her here at the bank. His mind kept wandering down the hallway to her office where he imagined her sitting, her soft, expressive hands working the computer keyboard, or holding the telephone, her eyes scanning information, her voice speaking, that voice he relished when it spoke his name, and thanked him for every small thing he did for her.

She was his love. But he just might have to recommend she be fired from her job.

twenty-four

"Chryssie, I have a favor to ask of you."

"Sure, Mom. What is it?"

It was a week before Thanksgiving and mother and daughter, along with three other women, were in the church basement sorting through shelves of canned goods and boxes of food for what would be used to provide a Thanksgiving dinner for the homeless in the area.

C.G. and Jane Grady were part of the Helping Hands ministry which collected food, clothing, and medical supplies throughout the year for the needy. C.G. particularly enjoyed helping at Thanksgiving and Christmas.

"I don't want you to say no until you've heard everything I have to say."

Properly warned, C.G. agreed.

"You know I've been trying to get you to meet a certain man whom I think you would like."

"Yes, Mom."

"You have steadfastly resisted my efforts."

"Yes, Mom."

Jane Grady put some cans of pumpkin pie mix down on a nearby table and faced her daughter. "Chryssie, I'm asking you, for my sake, to just meet this man once."

"Mom. . ."

"I'm embarrassed that you've been so stubborn. His mother is a good friend of mine, and I hate to keep telling her that I'm getting no cooperation from you."

C.G. gave her mom a hug, then stepped back and looked at her. "I'm not doing this to be difficult. Honestly. I know you think this man would be good for me, but I've told you I'm seeing someone, and we're pretty serious."

"Then why haven't your father or I met him?"

"We just want to be sure, so we're taking it one day at a time. I think soon I'll be able to bring him to the house to meet you."

Jane Grady looked so crestfallen that C.G. felt sorry for her. She imagined it hadn't been easy for her to constantly tell her friend that her daughter showed no interest in her son. It also showed disrespect for her mother's wishes.

"Mom, you told me once this man doesn't really want to meet me either."

"Well. . .yes. . .he's very busy with a project at work that leaves him almost no time at all for a social life. That's the reason, probably. But his mother feels just as strongly as I do that once you meet each other, you'll find common ground. She's most impressed by you."

"I've never met her."

"I've described you to her."

"Dare I ask what you said?"

Jane Grady patted C.G. on the cheek. "I simply told her the truth, that you are marvelous, and bright, and loving, and sophisticated. What man in his right mind wouldn't want you?"

"Don't you think that was a bit of oversell, Mom?"

"Absolutely not. In any case, I just wish you would consent to meeting him. For lunch. That's all. Nothing major. Just lunch." She gave C.G. a pleading look. "Just lunch. How bad could that be?"

C.G. sighed. "Okay, Mom, I'll meet him, but just for lunch."

"Oh, Chryssie," her mother exclaimed, her eyes bright with excitement, "that's wonderful. Thank you. I'll set it up. I wouldn't be surprised if someday you thank me for being so stubborn about this."

"We're talking lunch here, Mom, not marriage for life."

"I'll call my friend, Katherine, and set it up," her mother gushed. "Oh, she'll be so pleased."

They hugged each other, and C.G. decided not to confide that the only reason she'd agreed to see the man was to end her mother's silly maneuvering once and for all. She'd meet him, report no interest at all, and that would be the end of it.

She, of course, wanted no other man but Drake. They were

closer than ever, away from work, but at the bank, the tension between them was worsening, and Drake was being more and more friendly with James Wyatt. C.G. didn't want to think why.

It was only later when she was home that C.G. realized she didn't even know the man's name. It didn't matter, though, because he wasn't going to be a part of her life, not when she was in love with Drake Forrest, and was going to marry him.

Yes, she'd known she wanted to marry him for weeks now, but still thought it too soon to make such a major commitment. If their love for each other was real, and lasting, it could stand the test of a few more months of waiting.

She felt sorry for her mother, though, who really believed her friend's son was the man for her. C.G. hoped she would not be too disappointed when it didn't work out the way she'd wanted.

*

"Drake, Drake, you'll never guess what's going to happen."

Katherine Forrest was at her son's apartment, having brought him some sour cream chocolate cake. She'd also invited him home for Thanksgiving dinner. Her brother and sister-in-law and their two children, Drake's teenage cousins, were going to be there, too. They all got along well, and it would be an enjoyable day.

"What's going to happen, mother?" Drake asked, trying to decide which he enjoyed most, the rich chocolaty taste of the cake itself, or the old-fashioned fudge icing with which it was frosted.

"Jane's daughter has finally agreed to meet you."

Drake choked on a big chunk of cake that slipped down the wrong way. This endless project of his mother's to match him up with a friend's daughter was getting on his nerves.

He was in love with C.G. Grady and was going to marry C.G. Grady. He knew she wanted the same thing, although she had still not agreed to be his wife.

They'd spent nearly every evening together for months now, and had discovered their similarities and differences and had survived a few disagreements. Most importantly, they now shared the same faith.

"Did you hear what I said, Drake?" Katherine Forrest went on.

"Jane's daughter, Chryssie, has agreed to have lunch with you."

"Is that her name—Chryssie?" He snorted and gave his mother a discouraging look. "Sounds like a Barbie doll, Mother, not a real, live woman."

"Chryssie's not like that at all," Katherine persisted. "She's very intelligent and has a prestigious job. In computers. Just like you."

Drake groaned. "But Mother, I've told you I'm seeing someone now and it's serious."

"Oh? Then why haven't your father and I met her?"

"You will. Soon. We're just taking a little time to be sure it's right."

"In the meantime, though, won't you agree to meet with Chryssie? It's only for lunch. Just lunch. Oh, Drake, I've worked for months on this. You can't turn me down now."

Drake gave her a bear hug. After chocolate cake and cold milk, how could a man say no to his mother? "All right, I'll have lunch with this Chryssie person, but only on the condition that you understand it's just for lunch. Don't go making honeymoon reservations for us in Hawaii."

"Drake, don't be ridiculous." She smiled. "Actually, you might prefer the Caribbean."

"I'll decide on the restaurant," Drake said firmly.

"Fine."

He took his mother by the shoulders and gave her a special look of indulgent love. "I'm sorry you're going to be disappointed in this meeting, Mother, because you will be. I'm in love with the most wonderful woman in the world, and her name is not Chryssie."

❧

In her hand C.G. held the Final Implementation Plan that Drake had given her, right on time, as everything he did was right on time.

He was an amazing man, and having worked with him these past four months, she had come to respect him tremendously and understand why he was in such demand by the top companies in the country. When he gave his word, he stood by it. When he made a decision, he made it happen.

He was not easy to work with, or forgiving of mistakes, or understanding of sloppy work, but he was fair, and worked harder than anyone else to complete a project on schedule.

She looked at the Plan again, she being the only one to have received it, not Dottie and James as they had the Proposed Plan.

The Final Plan included order documentation for the three phone companies they had to use and for the twelve branches, each of which would receive separate bills. Carefully itemized were the new billing numbers, circuit I.D. numbers, service order numbers, and the installation dates Drake had ordered.

Additionally there were the billing numbers for the old analog circuits, their circuit I.D. numbers, disconnect order number, and the date service was to be disconnected. Impressive. Perfect.

The word "perfect" made her think of the man her mother had been trying to get her together with. Well, today, her wish was coming true: C.G. was meeting him for lunch at The Magnolia Tree, a charming, downtown restaurant with a reputation for excellent and innovative cuisine. He had suggested it, through his mother, through her mother to her, and C.G. gave him credit for having good taste.

She'd worn a lightweight ivory wool suit with fabric buttons down the front and at the wrists. The jacket was long and slimming, looked just as nice unbuttoned, and was accented by a gold lapel pin at the shoulder in the shape of a rose. Matching gold earrings shone to advantage, for her hair was swept back in a tiny French twist with a small gold comb at its base.

She hadn't dressed up for him, for the suit was one she often wore to the office, but she did want to look her best, for the sake of her mother.

C.G. went to the rest room, checked her makeup, and added a dab of perfume behind both ears. Why she was nervous she did not know, for this was going to be the first and last lunch she would have with Mr. Perfect.

Back in her office, she took her purse out of the drawer and withdrew her car keys from it.

She did not notice that Drake's Final Implementation Plan was not in the same position it had been in when she'd left.

twenty-five

Walking out to her car, C.G. realized she was dreading this lunch, wishing she had never agreed to meet this man. What could possibly come from it except her mother being disappointed that the two of them would not become a couple?

Because she'd lost the picture her mom had sent her of him, and had not received another, she had no idea what he looked like. Interestingly, though, his name was Drake. She had never known a Drake in her life, and now she was in love with one and about to meet another.

She wondered if this Drake was as embarrassed about the matchmaking as she was and would be just as glad as she when this obligatory lunch was over.

It only took her five minutes to drive to the downtown square, and parking was easy. She entered the restaurant, a small but elegant place with crisp honey-gold tablecloths, matching napkins, fresh flowers in delicate vases, and fifties music playing softly in the background.

When she gave her name, she was shown to a table by the hostess who told her her companion would arrive soon. "He's just called to say he will be delayed, but only shortly."

"Thank you."

C.G. sat down in the corner booth and the hostess asked, "Would you like anything to drink while you wait?"

"Just water, please. With lemon."

The hostess walked away and C.G. took a deep breath, almost glad she had another moment or two to compose herself.

In her single life she had had two blind dates, and while neither had been disastrous, both had been boring to the point she would have enjoyed herself more being at home watching Sesame Street.

Her water arrived, and she sipped it gratefully, her throat

suddenly dry. Looking slowly around the room, from one table to another, she speculated on the life's story of each person. She even tried putting names to the jolly grandmother, the pouty teenager, the shy, dark-haired beauty whose hand was being held by a man with red hair.

At the front of the restaurant she saw her hostess talking to someone, and when the man stepped around her, C.G. gasped.

It was Drake.

She choked on her water and spilled a little when she set the glass down with a clunk on the table.

How can I explain what I'm doing here, she thought in panic. *Will he believe that I'm meeting a man for lunch in whom I have absolutely no interest?*

She hurriedly picked up the large menu and put it in front of her face, but it was too late. He'd seen her, and was coming toward her table.

"C.G., what are you doing here?"

Picking up on the vehemence in his voice, she slowly lowered the menu and prepared to tell her implausible story when she was stopped by the look of raw fury on his face. Every muscle along his cheekbones was taut, as was the hard line of his mouth across his teeth. His eyes blazed; his nostrils were flared.

"Drake, what's the matter with you? What's happened?"

His eyes bored into her. "The game is over, Mata Hari." The words cut sharper than any knife could have.

C.G. started to get up, but Drake pushed her back down, a powerful hand digging into her shoulder. The look he pierced her with she never wanted to see again. It was hard, and almost cruel, and it told her that she was in serious trouble. But why?

"What made you do it?" he growled, leaning over her, his face only inches from her own, "Why did you risk your reputation, as well as mine?"

C.G. was speechless, having no idea what he was talking about.

"Well, I'm here to inform you that you didn't get away with it. You've been found out, and believe me when I say that I'll see to it you never work another day in this business again!"

C.G. gulped and her mouth fell open in disbelief at what she was hearing. She had never seen Drake so angry, and threatening.

Pushing his hand from her shoulder, she said as steadily as she could, "You'd better explain what you're talking about, because I haven't a clue."

"Really? Try explaining why you want to sabotage the acquisition."

"What?"

He sat down beside her, close, and she could feel the warmth of his breath on her cheeks. "You're good, C.G., very good. That innocent look you wear so effectively perfectly covers your deceit."

"Drake, just tell me what you're talking about." She was getting frustrated and annoyed at being accused of some horrendous crime of which she had absolutely no knowledge. She was also amazed and disappointed that Drake could think her guilty of something so terrible.

"The installation dates of the new circuits—why did you change them?"

"I didn't. Good heavens, why would I? That's your responsibility."

Drake glared at her, and slammed his arm across the back of the booth in a gesture C.G. could only assume was his way of telling her she could not escape him. But why would she want to?

A muscle twitched just below his right eye and the hand that lay on the table flexed and did not relax.

"I have proof that you called the three phone companies we're working with and changed the installation dates of the new circuits."

"Proof? That's impossible, because I did not call anyone."

"When I contacted the companies to verify that the circuits would be installed on the dates I ordered, I was told they'd been changed. 'By whom?' I asked each of the service reps."

"Do you mean someone can change those dates over the phone?"

Drake grunted. "Oh no, one must have written verification

for a new installation date request."

C.G. straightened her back and looked him straight on. "They did not get that from me, Drake."

He leaned even closer. "Oh, yes they did, Miss Grady. Each of the service reps has on file a fax from you, signed by you, on Ashford Bank and Trust stationery."

C.G. felt like she'd been stabbed. She could hardly breathe. "That's. . .that's impossible."

"I saw them. All three requests, with your signature, which I compared with others I got from your secretary, Greta."

She knew Drake was barely holding his temper. He looked as though he hated her, and she understood why. If the change had not been caught in time, there would have been chaos, not to mention that his reputation would have been seriously damaged, if not ruined altogether.

He thought she'd betrayed him, so she understood his rage, but she also knew he loved her, and shouldn't he be believing her, and trying to find out what really happened?

Tears gathered in her eyes and slid down her cheeks.

"Oh, please," he roared, and nearby customers looked up, startled. "Don't play the poor, wrongly-accused woman with me."

Suddenly the anger left him, and anguish took its place. "How could you have done this to me, C.G.? To your own bank?" He looked as though *he* were going to cry any moment, and her spirit rallied a little at the realization that he still cared and was trying to figure out what had happened.

She reached out, and put her hands on both sides of his face. "Drake, believe me, I did not do this. I can't explain it. I don't know how the phone companies got my signature on the letters, but it was not from me." She said the last words slowly, with great emphasis.

Drake grabbed her wrists and hung on tightly. "No one, C.G., and I mean no one, interferes with my work and gets away with it."

Flinging her hands away from him, he sprang to his feet, but leaned back over the table and glared at her. "I don't know why you made me fall in love with you—"

"Made you?" C.G. cried, scooting out of the booth and bravely confronting him. "*Made* you? If I remember correctly, Mr. Forrest, you were the one who decided you felt that way about me, almost as soon as you met me, while I was trying to keep my distance from you."

"A clever game, obviously."

"It was no game, and you know it. You've just rededicated your life to the Lord. How can you judge me so harshly? So unfairly? I'm a sister in Christ."

"I have facts!" he roared, and pounded the table with one fist, rattling the dishes and sending one coffee cup crashing to the floor. "You betrayed me!"

The hostess hurried over to them and said firmly, "Please leave our restaurant and continue your argument somewhere else."

C.G. gasped in extreme embarrassment and covered her mouth with her hand. She felt sick to her stomach. Turning, she ran from the restaurant without looking back, praying Drake would not follow her.

She ran all the way to her car, and drove to the bank with tears streaming down her cheeks, not even realizing she had abandoned lunch with her mother's friend's son.

In her mind she heard, over and over, Drake's stinging words: "You betrayed me! You betrayed me!"

She wanted to go home. How could she go back into the bank after what had happened? Who else knew what Drake had just told her?

Her heart was pounding fearfully when she entered the doors, and she walked on unsteady legs toward her office. No one gaped at her; the tellers paid no attention; even Greta gave her a cheerful "Hi, how was lunch?"

At her desk, she collapsed into her chair just at the moment she knew she could not take another step. Her breathing was shallow and her face was bathed in sweat.

She half expected Drake to come barging into the bank, into her office, and continue his diatribe against her. But he didn't come.

Ten minutes went by before C.G. felt in control of herself. She was ashamed of her unprofessional argument with Drake, in public no less, and wished she could have stood up to him without tears, but she hadn't.

How was she going to convince Drake that the "proof" he had was not reliable?

Then another cold, deadly thought struck her mind: Someone had written three letters in her name requesting changes of dates on the installation of the circuits.

Someone had forged her signature.

Someone wanted to destroy her career.

twenty-six

The ringing of the phone jarred C.G. from her thoughts on the incredible realization that someone was playing with her career.

"C.G., this is Gerald Ramey. Please come to my office immediately." The phone went dead with an ominous click, and C.G. knew what was coming.

With zombie-like steps she made her way to the large, corner office of the bank's president, a tall, heavily built man with thinning white hair, with whom she had always gotten along well. She listened to him accuse her of the heinous act of sabotage.

He showed her the faxed letters under her signature, and C.G. had to admit they looked genuine.

Though Mr. Ramey did give her a chance to defend herself, he sternly concluded, "In the face of this irrefutable evidence that Drake Forrest has brought me, I have no choice but to relieve you of all responsibility for the Information Systems Division."

She was fired.

"Please gather your personal belongings and leave the bank immediately," the president said.

C.G. stared at him. "But sir, I'm willing to stay a few weeks until you find someone else, or until I can prove my innocence."

He did not smile at her but stood to his feet behind his desk, and from the uncompromising expression on his face, C.G. knew the matter was decided. There was no hope of understanding. And she couldn't blame him. If a man with the reputation of Drake Forrest reported such a contemptible act by a bank employee, what else could be done but to get the traitor off the premises immediately?

"Mr. Ramey, I am not guilty of what I'm accused of," she told him one last time. "Please let me stay and try to clear my name."

"No, Miss Grady. But I can promise you there will be a full-scale investigation, and if you are found innocent, you will be contacted." Then his eyes became kinder. "You have been an outstanding employee up to this time. We thank you for all your efforts on behalf of Ashford Bank and Trust. Good-bye." He did not offer her his hand.

It took C.G. thirty minutes to clear her desk and credenza of personal things, for she could not get herself to move quickly. Dottie and James came in, aghast at what had happened, both offering to quit, in protest, but she insisted they stay and help Drake.

"How can you want us to help your enemy?" Dottie cried.

"I'm going to punch him in the nose," James said, and when C.G. imagined the skinny, underdeveloped James taking on the formidable, muscled Drake, she almost laughed, but didn't. James meant what he said; he wanted to defend her, and she appreciated his support more than she could tell him.

She gave each of her two assistants a hug and said, "I don't know how I'm going to prove my innocence, but I swear to you that I did not do what I'm accused of."

"Of course you didn't," Dottie insisted, "and believe me, C.G., James and I will do everything we can here to find out the truth and get you reinstated."

They left, and C.G. was ready to leave, too, but there was one more thing she had to do: she had to go and see Drake.

Drake heard her open his door and come into his office, and he dreaded looking up. His heart was a twisted mass of agony and he didn't know how to deal with his love for C.G. and his fury at her betrayal of him. *Why, Lord? Why?* he questioned.

"Drake, I. . .I came to say good-bye."

He stood up and wasn't prepared for the anguish he saw etched on her usually serene features. Though her face clearly showed where rivulets of tears had slid over her cheeks, she had never looked more beautiful to him—like a martyr going to her death, which was an apt description for, because of him, she had just experienced the death of her career. Mr. Ramey had called him the minute he'd finished with C.G. and told him she'd been fired.

It had taken all of Drake's willpower not to rush to her office and take her in his arms and tell her it was all right, that he knew it was a terrible mistake, that he would find who had done this vile thing, and would make her life right again. He had wanted to do that, but he hadn't. Facts were facts, and he had the evidence on his desk. C.G. was guilty!

Warring against his noble nature that insisted this woman he loved was an angel who would never betray him and her bank, was the dark side of his nature that ridiculed him for being a sucker, falling in love with a woman he barely knew, getting involved with the church he'd abandoned years ago.

Satan put him on the rack and made him question his new commitment, C.G.'s spirituality, and where God had been when this "crime" had been perpetrated against him and his employer.

In an instant of time, all these thoughts crashed through his head, vying for supremacy, and Drake was more confused and angry than he could ever remember being.

He was a man who would not be made a fool of, and C.G. Grady had done exactly that. Fortunately, he had discovered her act before havoc had been created among the many branches of the two banks involved.

Now she was here, daring to face him. She was saying good-bye.

"Good-bye, Miss Grady."

Those were the only words he could say. The only safe ones. He wanted to rail at her; he wanted to tell her he adored her.

She gave him a tiny little smile that broke his heart and said quietly, "I have no explanation for what happened, but as God is my Savior, Drake, I did not do it."

"Stop it! Don't bring God into this as your witness."

He wanted to throw something, physically vent his wrath at the impossibility of what had happened.

But it had happened, and he could not look C.G. in the eye, but turned his back to her and folded his arms across his chest.

There was not a sound in the room. The very air stopped moving and Drake thought he would never breathe again.

Then he heard the click of his door being closed, and he

whirled around, and found the space where she'd been standing empty. She was gone. Out of his office. Out of his life.

"Oh, God," he groaned, covering his face with his hands, "what is the truth here?" He waited for a thunderbolt from heaven to tell him, but all that he heard was the silence.

In his apartment that night, Drake forgot to turn on the lights, and he sat in his great room, alone, in the shadows, in total quiet, and wondered what he could do to make the numbness go away.

He hadn't eaten all day. He was lethargic one minute and restless the next. The loss he felt was excruciating for it attacked him personally as well as professionally.

"Why, C.G.? Why?" he moaned.

Leaning over, his hands on his knees, he gazed down at the carpet, searching for meaning out of the worst day in his life.

None of it made sense. What could possibly be C.G.'s motive for doing such a crazy thing?

First of all, she was a Christian, a genuine, loving follower of the Lord. He wouldn't have thought her capable of such deceit. Could she have fooled him all these months into thinking she was honest and trustworthy? Wouldn't he have seen any deviation in her behavior, sensed a frustration or anger or greed that would drive her to betray her own bank, and him?

Secondly, she was an intelligent woman, organized and logical in her thinking. Surely, she must have known she'd be caught either before or after the crisis. Her signature was on the letters, for Pete's sake. It had been child's play for him to find it.

He stood up and paced the room in a frenzy then, running his hands repeatedly through his hair. "She's innocent. She has to be. C.G.'s too smart to have done such a dumb thing. Too clever."

He stopped and studied the empty fireplace which was swept clean of winter's ashes. "So, if *she's* not guilty, then who is dumb enough to pull a stunt like this?" he questioned. "Who wants to hurt C.G.?"

He determined to find out.

C.G. waited till the next day to tell her parents the unbelievable story of what had happened to her at the bank. She also apologized to her mother for not keeping the date with her friend's son.

"Sweetheart, how terrible for you," her mother moaned, taking her child in her arms, and comforting her. "Why don't you come home for a few days? Let us take care of you while you're hurting."

C.G. drew back and smiled appreciatively. "I'm a grown woman, Mom. I have to take care of myself."

"Which you do admirably. But not now, when you're wounded, when you need time to recuperate, and forgive."

"Forgive?"

"Yes, forgive that horrible man who got you fired, forgive the bank for not standing by you. Forgive, or this can destroy you, eat away your self-confidence, strip you of ambition to succeed."

"Oh, Mom, at what am I supposed to succeed? My career is ruined. No bank will ever hire me, or any other institution."

Mrs. Grady took her daughter to a gleaming, waist-high walnut table upon which sat a huge, old family Bible from the 1800's. "This was your great-grandfather's," she said to C.G., opening the heavy, ornate, leather cover. "Read what he wrote there in 1898."

C.G. leaned over the Bible she'd seen all the days of her life, and read words she'd read many times before, in the hand of a man she'd never known: "There is no problem that cannot be solved by reading this book."

She sighed and closed the cover and turned to her mother. "I know that's true, and I know some passages I need to review that will help me through this."

Jane Grady smiled. "Then stay with us a few days, and study. Find peace here in what used to be your home."

C.G. finally agreed, and walked a little quicker up the familiar stairs to the sage and peach-colored room that once had been hers, in which she'd grown from a little girl to a young lady, and had left when she'd gone away to college in another city.

Her parents used it now for a guest room, and even though it didn't have her knickknacks on the dresser and her wild animal posters on the wall, it was still her room, and her mind flooded with poignant memories of happy days spent here.

She sank down on the bed, stared up at the ceiling, and whispered, "Dear God, I don't know what to do. I don't know if I can forgive Drake. Guide me, please." Then a tremendous sob escaped her mouth, and she cried herself to sleep.

twenty-seven

The few days C.G. had originally planned to spend with her parents extended longer, as her mother persuaded her to help with a Christmas party she was having for her church missionary group and her father told her he'd missed their nightly chess games.

With no job, no income, no man to love, and Christmas only two weeks away, C.G. faced the holiday with little enthusiasm. Even decorating her parents' house, shopping with her mother for gifts, caroling door-to-door with the singles group from church, and being constantly reminded by jingles on the radio and television that this was the season to be jolly, she was sad and discouraged. Nothing in her life was going right, and she didn't know why.

Steadfastly she read her great-grandfather's Bible, and prayed for wisdom. She found comfort in many of David's Psalms written when he'd been oppressed and misunderstood, pursued by enemies and treacherous family.

One of the most comforting was from Psalm 27:11-14: "Teach me Your way, O Lord, and lead me in a smooth path, because of my enemies. Do not deliver me to the will of my adversaries; for false witnesses have risen against me, and such as breathe out violence. I would have lost heart, unless I had believed that I would see the goodness of the Lord in the land of the living. Wait on the Lord; be of good courage, and He shall strengthen your heart; wait, I say, on the Lord!"

Just as David had believed that God was his deliverer, his light, and his salvation, C.G. also clung to that belief, knowing that God was walking with her through this dark valley.

She hadn't heard from Drake since the day she had been fired, and the temptation to call him or go to his apartment was almost overpowering at times, but she had enough pride not to throw herself at him. His love for her had not been strong enough for him to believe in her innocence, no matter what the evidence against her, and accepting this appalling fact was particularly hurtful.

Though she'd been looking for a job with any eligible company from Atlanta to north Georgia, C.G. had been unsuccessful. The question inevitably posed by the interviewer, "Why did you leave your last position?" was a painful one to answer honestly, and though she'd been tempted to simply say she'd quit, she knew she could not out-and-out lie. No one wanted her.

She didn't give up trying to clear her name, and made some calls or went to the various phone companies in an attempt to talk with someone who could help her discover who had falsely represented her.

Each party would not talk with her, and though they displayed various reactions to her story, from sympathy to disbelief, she learned nothing from them, until one day, during her second visit to the friendliest service representative, who said to her, "You know, your voice sounds different in person than it did on the phone when you first called about changing the installation date."

"How do you mean?" C.G.'s heart began to race.

"You sounded much older then, and. . .grouchier. Like you were having a bad day." What older woman could have called the phone company and impersonated her? C.G. pondered. She went through all the possibilities, and none of them made sense.

What if it were a younger woman, just trying to sound older? That introduced a whole new set of characters, and at the top of the list was Susie Black, except that C.G. just didn't think Susie had the knowledge to pull off something so complicated.

She called Dottie at the bank and Dottie agreed. Discussing various candidates, neither could think of someone who would want to destroy C.G.

"You were one of the most popular people here," Dottie insisted, in frustration. "It's been awful without you."

From Dottie, C.G. learned that the acquisition took place on schedule, the equipment changes were implemented without a problem, and that Drake Forrest was only at the bank one or two days a week. "Troubleshooting mostly. James and I are handling the workload until they hire someone to take your place, but the bank personnel see now that that isn't going to be easy. You were a whiz."

There was an awkward silence and then Dottie added, "Oh, phooey, I'm going to stick my nose into your business and ask, have you heard from Drake at all?"

"No, Dottie, I haven't."

"The bum. How could he turn on you like he did? Not believe in you?"

"He could have lost his reputation over what almost happened."

"And that's more important than believing in the woman you love and fighting for her?"

"Dottie, I really don't want to talk about this."

"Sure, sure. But listen, I've been doing some snooping around here, and I have an idea who the troublemaker is."

"You do?"

"I'll get back to you in a few days. I may need your help."

"Oh, Dottie, I'll do anything to clear my name."

"Remember that statement."

"Well, almost anything," C.G. amended.

ஃ

Drake's mouth went dry when he got the phone call from his mother: "Your father has had a stroke, dear. The doctor says it will be touch and go for a few days. Can you come home?"

"Of course. I'm on my way."

Mr. Forrest made it through the dangerous days, and was allowed to go home from the hospital a week later. Drake spent as much time as he could with his parents, but it was not easy. The bank acquisition had taken place as scheduled, and his work there was nearly finished, but still required at least a couple days a week to be sure things stayed on track.

In addition, he had just signed a contract worth hundreds of thousands of dollars with an Atlanta brokerage firm that would keep him and his firm involved in the latest technology for at least two years.

He was back to his old, familiar grind of working day and night to keep life on target, except he still made time for church, prayer, and Bible study. And, he'd had more than one talk with Pastor Horton about C.G.

He knew he needed strength beyond his own to carry him through, and that God would provide.

He missed working with the people at Ashford Bank and Trust, now part of the Georgia National Bank family. After C.G. had been fired, Dottie and James, particularly James, had been a big help to him. In fact, every time he'd turned around, there was James, volunteering to do something, anything to get on his good side.

It hadn't taken many such occasions for Drake to realize what James wanted: C.G.'s job.

Losing C.G. was something Drake still had not gotten over, even though at first, when he'd been faced with evidence that she had betrayed him, he was sure he'd never forgive her or want to speak to her again.

Since those early days, he'd thought endlessly about it, coming eventually to the conclusion that C.G. could not possibly have done what he'd blamed her for.

Painstakingly he'd tried to find out who the real guilty party was, doing so as carefully as he could without arousing suspicion. It had not been easy; the person had covered his or her tracks well.

Drake wanted desperately to see C.G., to let her know he was working to exonerate her, but he didn't want to give her false hope and take her through more pain if he wasn't successful.

As difficult as it was to stay away from her, he made himself do so, praying all the time that she'd still be there when he came to rescue her.

Now he was facing another crisis: Not many days after his father got home from the hospital, his mother fell in the driveway, and broke her kneecap.

Her mending rendered her immobile, in a plaster cast from ankle to hip, in which she would stay for ten days or so, and then she'd be put in a fiberglass cast for at least another two months. The doctor told Drake that total healing could take up to a year.

"When is it all going to stop, Lord?" Drake prayed more than once, feeling intensely the buffeting of the storm around him. He was not enjoying the Christmas season at all.

He moved home to help out: cooking, cleaning, fixing, decorating for Christmas, and buying gifts. He was frazzled, and what time he could give, away from his several business requirements, was pitifully inadequate. He determined to hire some temporary help.

"Oh, you don't have to do that, dear," his mother told him when he approached her with the idea. "The church is going to start sending in food three days a week, and someone to clean."

"You're kidding."

She smiled. "Being a Christian is more than sitting in a pew one hour a week."

"I know, but that's a lot to do for you and Dad."

"It's a service the people are happy to give, in Christ's name."

With relief, Drake went off to work each day, and returned home to find nourishing food in the refrigerator, the house sparkling clean, and his father and mother mending. How blessed his parents were to have their lives surrounded by a "family" of believers who cared about each other.

If only he could mend C.G.'s life.

twenty-eight

"Chryssie, I have a favor to ask of you."

It was nine o'clock in the morning, three days before Christmas, and Jane Grady was dashing about the house scooping up wrapping paper, ribbons, and bows, and stuffing them into a huge shopping bag to take to the church to use for decorating the gifts to be given to the Sunday school children.

"I was supposed to go to a friend's house today to clean. Her husband's had a stroke, and she's broken her kneecap. Can you believe it? But I forgot I'm also to be at the church to help wrap gifts. It's an all-day activity."

"Say no more, Mom; I'll be happy to pinch-hit for you. What's the address?"

While C.G. was, indeed, happy to help out her mother, she hated the fact that she had the time to do so. She still didn't have a job, and future prospects were grim. It was hard to get into the Christmas spirit, though she tried not to let her frustration show and concern her parents.

Her mother handed her a piece of paper. "Katherine will appreciate anything you can do, dear. She's a good friend."

C.G. smiled. Her mother had dozens of good friends, for she was a charming woman whose style and grace, as well as caring nature, just made people want to be around her.

C.G. came to realize that this friend, however, was different from the others. The first hint came at the front door when the attractive woman on crutches, in her mid-fifties with ash-blond hair, introduced herself as Katherine Forrest. The last name touched a tender spot in C.G.'s heart, and she battled not to be overwhelmed with remorse that she and Drake Forrest were no longer together.

Every day she half expected to hear from him, but in the weeks since she'd left the bank, he had neither called nor written, and she knew this because she went back to her house often to check her mailbox and telephone answering machine.

The second indication that Katherine Forrest was, indeed, a good friend of her mother's, a very good friend, came when C.G. was dusting the master bedroom. There, on the dresser, was a picture of a strikingly handsome man in tennis togs, with the racket held firmly in front of him, and a determined look on his face.

C.G. found herself staring at Drake Forrest.

"Oh, no," she groaned out loud. "This can't be his parents' home." She remembered Drake telling her they lived in the city, and he had mentioned the street, but she had forgotten it, until now, until she found herself in the parental home of the man who had destroyed her career unjustly.

She wanted to pick up the picture and throw it through the window. She wanted to pick up the picture and hold it to her heart. Instead, she finished the housework and fixed a light lunch for Mr. and Mrs. Forrest who were kind and appreciative and made it easy to see where Drake got his loving side.

Every time C.G. looked at Katherine Forrest she saw Drake, for their facial features and coloring were similar. It was from his father that he got his gruffness of manner and the straight set of his shoulders.

She stayed longer than she'd expected, doing this and that, her reason being, honestly, to help these unfortunate people. Added to that, though she wouldn't have admitted it, was the bittersweet experience of feeling Drake's presence. Did she still love him? Or despise him?

"He was an easy child to raise," Katherine Forrest told C.G. about Drake, not knowing the two of them knew each other, and well. The two women were in the small white and blue kitchen with its collection of teapots sitting on a long shelf above the cabinets, and C.G. was fixing the older woman a cup of tea.

"Even as a child Drake understood the adult mind. All we had to do was explain why we were saying no or yes, and he reasoned it out for himself that it was in his best interest to trust us. That doesn't mean he didn't have a temper, or want his own way occasionally." Mrs. Forrest laughed lightly. "I can show you the closet door he put his fist through one time."

C.G. looked surprised.

"He's been very good to us, and we're proud of his success. Even though he's extremely busy these days with a new client, he stays here as much as he can and does all kinds of things for us. Bless his heart. He offered to hire some temporary help, but we really don't need it with him being here, and the church helping as it does."

She gave C.G. an especially warm smile. "Jane, of course, has been a real blessing, and we appreciate all she's done for us, and for sending you to us, Chryssie. You've been a dear today, giving us far more time than you should have."

"I was happy to do so, Mrs. Forrest."

"You really should meet my son, Drake. The two of you would hit it off, I'm sure." She looked at her watch. "In fact, he should be here any minute."

C.G. caught her breath. The possibility of Drake finding her there sent her temperature rising.

"If there's nothing else you need me for today, then I'll go," she anxiously told Mrs. Forrest, suddenly desperate to be gone.

For weeks she'd been wanting to see Drake, talk to him, see if he'd had a change of heart, but since she had not heard one word from him, the prospect of being face-to-face with the man who had not believed her and had caused her firing, made her intensely uncomfortable.

She had prayed for the courage to forgive him; seeing him in person would tell her whether or not she had been able to. Only she didn't really want to see him.

"Please call my mother, or me, if there's anything at all you need," she said to Katherine Forrest who squeezed her hands and said, "You're an angel. I wish my son would find someone as wonderful as you to love." There was a decided twinkle in her eye, and C.G. wondered if she ever played matchmaker as her own mother was doing.

After a quick good-bye, she was out the door, brushing tears from her eyes as she scurried toward her car.

Deep in thought over her own troubles, and looking down at the sidewalk, she did not hear the footsteps approaching until she ran right into...someone. Powerful hands grasped her shoulders to keep her from falling, and when she looked up, she almost fainted.

It was Drake.

"C.G.? What are you doing here?"

The sound of his voice sent a thrill through her. The strength of his hands almost made her forget what he had done.

Straightening herself, she backed away from his support and looked into the intense blue eyes of the man she thought she had known so well. They drew her to him as deeply as his words, but she knew there was no point in dreaming of a love that no longer was possible.

"I did some work for your folks."

"What kind of work?"

"Light housework. Straightening up. Lunch."

Drake looked puzzled. "Why are you doing that? Mother said some folks from the church would be cleaning and cooking."

"It was my mother's request. She was going to help your folks today, but then couldn't, so she asked me to instead. Since I have nothing better to do. . ."

The words hung in the air and Drake commented, "No, that's not what you're trained for, is it?"

Not knowing what to say to that remark, or being up to having an altercation with him, C.G. stepped around him and started again for her car.

Drake followed. "C.G., I want you to know how sorry I am about what happened at the bank."

She whirled around and stared at him. "You're sorry? Now, you say you're sorry? I could have used your sympathy and understanding back then. I was innocent, but couldn't convince you of that, and I haven't been able to find any proof to clear my name. So, Mr. Forrest, I'm unemployable at the moment, thanks to you being so sure I was the one who tried to sabotage the acquisition. For a man who told me you loved me, you sure didn't stick around when the going got tough."

She fumbled with her key, trying to unlock the car door, but her hands wouldn't cooperate. They were shaking.

Drake's hands covered hers, stopping her efforts. "C.G., we need to talk."

"I have nothing to say to you. Let me go."

Surprisingly, he did, and all the way home C.G. was torn between anger toward him for giving up on her so easily and her wishing they were together again.

"That's impossible," she said out loud, "and you'd better accept it, girl. Drake Forrest is out of your life forever."

twenty-nine

Drake longed to tell C.G. what he'd been piecing together about that tragedy of her losing her job, but he couldn't. Yet. The guilty party was not quite in the net.

The look on her face when she'd seen him seared his conscience. She had suffered professional humiliation and personal betrayal—both at his hands, and her tired, sad eyes betrayed her devastation. He wouldn't blame her if she never forgave him.

Despite her accusatory words, he had not felt venom from her. Only an honest asking of how he could have misjudged her so horribly. He didn't know himself.

Going into his parents' house, he listened to ten minutes of his mother's ravings about how wonderful "the Grady girl" was. He would have liked to have told her that he was in love with that Grady girl, wanted to marry her, and still would, as soon as certain things were worked out. And they would be worked out.

Katherine called Jane. "Your daughter is a jewel, and will be a perfect wife for my son."

"Thank you for thinking so. Between losing her job and her friendship with this man at work, the poor child has been suffering, and I didn't want to suggest another meeting with your son after their lunch date didn't materialize. But, with Christmas right around the corner, this may be the perfect time to get them together. After all, what season is more romantic and filled with hope than Christmas?"

"I agree. What shall we do?"

"Why not have them go with us to the community singing of *The Messiah* on Christmas Eve? Could you manage that, with your crutches?"

"Drake will help. Kevin can't go, of course, but my brother will be here visiting, and will keep him company."

"All right. Afterward, we could come back here for some refreshments."

"And find some way to leave the young people alone."

Jane Grady laughed. "Aren't we wicked, Katherine Forrest?"

"Not at all, Jane Grady. We're only doing what any self-respecting mother would do: Find the very best daughter- and son-in-law possible."

"Do you think we should tell them they'll be meeting each other?"

There was a long pause before Katherine said, "No."

They giggled and then prayed over the phone.

❧

"C.G., this is Dottie. You need to come down to the bank right away."

It was nine o'clock at night, two nights before Christmas.

"Why are you whispering? What's happening?"

"I'll explain when you get here. Park in the shopping center lot. Come to the side door." She hung up.

❧

It was humid and dark when C.G. stepped out of her car. Feeling strangely like a secret agent rendezvousing with a foreign spy, she walked cautiously toward the back of the bank. There were no cars in its parking lot.

She passed the drive-up window and arrived at the small side door employees used to come and go after hours.

It was armed with a security system, but she wouldn't have dreamed of punching in the numbers. That's all she needed to seal her criminal reputation forever—to be caught breaking into a bank where she no longer worked.

The door suddenly opened and a hand reached out and grabbed her inside. She started to scream until she saw that it was Dottie.

"Dottie! Why this cloak and dagger stuff?" C.G. questioned, feeling her skin start to crawl. She wasn't adventurous by nature.

"We don't want anyone to know we're here."

"Why?"

"Because we're going to find evidence on who framed you."

"We are?"

"Yes. Now go to James' office and wait for me. Don't turn the lights on. Keep the door open."

C.G. did as she was told, but her heart was pounding. What if someone else at the bank decided to work late? What if James came?

She got to his office and sat down on the only chair he had and tried to keep from fidgeting. She didn't like being there. With the lights off it was pitch dark, for there were no windows either facing the lobby or the outside of the building. She strained to listen for Dottie. What was this all about anyway?

The motion of a body passing by alerted her to the fact that someone had come into the office, and she jumped up to flee when she was caught—in the arms of Drake Forrest.

"What are you doing here?" she exclaimed, aghast. "Where's Dottie?"

"Here I am." The small lamp on the corner of James' desk was turned on, and C.G. blinked to adjust her vision.

"Why are we here?" C.G. asked. "Why is Drake here?"

"Because he and I think we know who the culprit is who cost you your job, C.G., and we're looking for evidence."

"You and Drake?"

Drake moved closer to her. "It seems Dottie and I have been working separately toward the same goal."

"Really?" So he did care. He believed in her after all. C.G.'s heart swelled with joy, and she thanked God for answering her prayer and almost burst out singing.

Drake swept her into his arms and gave her a long and hungry kiss then held her close. "I've missed you, C.G. Forgive me for not believing you right from the start."

"Come on, you two," Dottie said impatiently, "you can make up later. We have work to do."

C.G. couldn't leave the warmth of Drake's arms. Nothing else really mattered as long as he believed in her, knew she hadn't betrayed him. But this wasn't the time to mend fences.

"Yes, let's get on with it," she agreed, turning out of his embrace and hugging Dottie.

Nervously she looked over her shoulder, to the now-closed door, positive they would be caught at any moment. She definitely was not into breaking and entering, although technically they weren't doing that because Dottie was an employee, but it felt like it to her.

"What are we doing in James' office?" she asked. "I don't think he would take kindly to us being here."

Dottie grunted, "C.G., after I show you two files, you won't care a whit what James Wyatt thinks."

ⁿⁿ

Every year on Christmas Eve, the United Methodist Church of Cheston hosted a community sing-along of *The Messiah*. It was a treasured evening for the three-to-four hundred people who attended and sang the magnificent oratorio from well-worn copies.

The sanctuary was tastefully decorated with tall candles and sprigs of evergreen, and the pipe organ played Christmas hymns as people took their seats.

Jane and Jonathan Grady arrived with Chryssie and walked down the right aisle.

Katherine Forrest hobbled carefully down the left aisle, on her crutches, aided by her handsome son, Drake.

The Gradys went to the center section, the seventh row from the front.

Katherine Forrest pointed Drake to the seventh row, center section.

Jane Grady told Chryssie to go in first.

Katherine insisted Drake go in first.

The families met.

Drake and C.G.'s eyes found each other. Then they smiled.

Jane and Katherine hardly breathed, so intent were they on watching the looks on the faces of their children as they met for the first time. They just prayed that there would be an initial interest, a small spark that might grow, in time, into a significant love. They sighed as the fruition of their long months of matchmaking came to an end.

"C.G.," her mother said, "may I present the man I've been

telling you about. Drake Forrest."

"Drake, this is Chryssie Grady," Katherine Forrest introduced.

With a roguish smile, Drake leaned forward and lingeringly kissed C.G. on the cheek. "What a beautiful name—Chryssie. I've been looking forward to meeting you."

Katherine Forrest's eyes grew round.

"And I, you, Mr. Forrest. My mother tells me you are strong, dependable, adorable, protective. . .oh, yes," she leaned toward him, "and have mischievous eyes."

Jane Grady's eyebrows slid to the ceiling.

"I wonder if we're supposed to fall in love now, or wait till after the concert," Drake questioned, gazing at his mother whose mouth was strangely open.

"I'm afraid we'll have to wait, Drake darling," C.G. answered, "as the choir is entering, and the soloists."

Jane Grady sank into her chair, stunned.

C.G. and Drake sat down and reached out to each other, their hands locking while they gazed at each other in rapturous attention.

"I must say, Miss Grady, that my mother was absolutely correct when she described you as sophisticated and beautiful, smart, and possessing a peaches-and-cream complexion. You also sing?"

"Yes, I do."

"I'm anxious to hear you."

Katherine Forrest leaned forward to hear every word. Jane Grady leaned back and closed her eyes.

"How's it going?" Jonathan Grady asked his wife, glancing over at his daughter holding hands with a man he'd never met.

He received no answer. For once in their lives, Katherine Forrest and Jane Grady were speechless.

thirty

During intermission, the audience adjourned to a lovely fellowship hall where Christmas cookies and cakes, cheeses, and punch were being served.

"Excuse us, please," Drake said to the mothers and C.G.'s father, and before they had a chance to say anything, he whisked C.G. across the room, and through the first door he saw. It happened to be a clothes closet, a small clothes closet at that, with folding chairs stacked along one side. There was barely room for the two of them and the chairs.

"What are you—?" C.G.'s words were lost when Drake's mouth captured hers in an ardent and prolonged kiss. They clung together, relishing being together, and didn't hear the pounding on the door.

"Don't you think we should tell our mothers we finally figured out we are the object of their matchmaking?" C.G. suggested.

"Later." Drake caressed her face with his fingertips and gazed at her with intense emotion. "I can hardly believe everything worked out between us last night in the bank when Dottie called us in."

"And I'm grateful that finding those pages in James' office on which he practiced forging my signature, and copies of the new installation date requests he instigated, were enough to convince you, AND the bank president, that James, and not I, was the one who had tried to sabotage the acquisition."

"So he could get rid of you, and take your place."

"I still can't believe that timid James was so vicious."

"And that he was responsible for all the other mysterious things that happened, that I blamed you for."

"Like the wrong information sent to you that very first day, and the file I'd left on your desk which James claimed to accidentally have taken."

"The rat."

"Don't forget the figure changes he made in that report you asked both of us to do for you."

"And the wrong time being inserted onto your calendar that made you late for an important meeting with the four of us." Drake growled in disgust. "James always hated working for a woman."

"How do you know that?"

"I began to suspect there was more to James than we realized because he tried too hard to get on my good side. Once I figured he wanted your job, I became his buddy, continued to proclaim your guilt, and soon found out what a frustrated and angry young man he really is."

"But we always got along."

"You thought."

"For him to use his mother, as my voice, was really incredible. That one time I met her, I knew she wanted more success for her son, but I never would have guessed she would go to such lengths to obtain it."

"Fortunately, that one service rep you found a few weeks ago who thought your voice didn't match the one she'd heard the first time was willing to cooperate with the police, and recognized James' mother's voice as the one pretending to be you."

C.G. slipped her arms around Drake's waist and laid her head against his shoulder. "It's fortunate for me I had two people who loved me enough to work to clear my name."

"I can't accept any plaudits, C.G." Drake admitted, "because I was an insensitive jerk who was more concerned over my own ego and career than with yours. I should have known you could never do anything so dishonest."

He choked on the words and C.G. saw tears in his eyes that filled her with wonder at the depth of his caring.

"You were a true Christian, C.G., to forgive me as you did. Once I realized you had to be innocent, I prayed many long hours for wisdom to sort out the whole mess."

"I did, too." She touched his cheek tenderly. "Isn't it

comforting to know God was working in both our lives to bring us together?"

"With a little help from our mothers."

Drake drew her back into his arms and was kissing her thoroughly when the door was suddenly flung open and there stood their mothers.

"What are you two doing in there?" Katherine Forrest asked sharply.

"Getting acquainted, Mother, just as you wanted," Drake answered.

"You've barely been introduced," Jane Grady pronounced sternly. "C.G., please show some decorum. You're acting . . .common."

"I can't help it, Mom. You were right. He's everything I want in a man. In a husband."

"Husband?" Jane Grady exclaimed, gaping first at her daughter, then at her friend, Katherine, wondering what kind of calamity the two of them had unleashed.

Their plan had been to introduce Drake and Chryssie, have them like each other enough to start dating, and then a year later they could get married. Ending up in each other's arms in a clothes closet at church was not at all according to plan.

"Come out of there, please," Katherine Forrest ordered, and C.G. and Drake obeyed, still holding hands and trying to keep from laughing.

When they entered the fellowship hall, the two mothers threw anxious glances every direction to see if anyone they knew had seen their children coming out of a very small closet, flushed in the face, and hanging on to each other like newlyweds.

Just as the mothers began to breathe easier, Drake turned to C.G. and said, "Since we're going to get married, don't you think you should tell me your real name?"

"Married?" Katherine Forrest screeched.

Drake nodded, and C.G. did, too.

"It's Chrysanthemum Geraldine." She shuddered and Drake kept a perfectly straight face.

"Chrysanthemum Geraldine? What an unusual name."

"There's nothing wrong with it, young man," Jane Grady insisted.

"You're absolutely right, Mrs. Grady," Drake agreed. "May I ask why you chose it?" Now he understood why C.G. used C.G. at work. Imagine someone signing Chrysanthemum Geraldine Grady ten times a day, and who'd believe the name anyway?

"My husband and I," and she looked around her, but Jonathan Grady was nowhere to be seen, "named her Chrysanthemum because we met each other at a famous botanical garden in south Georgia, while walking through the chrysanthemum display."

"I see," Drake said, grateful they hadn't been in a rhubarb patch.

"Geraldine is my maternal grandmother's name."

"Thank you."

They noticed the people filing back into the sanctuary.

"We'd better go back in," Katherine said.

"Yes," Jane agreed, and they both started for the door but stopped when Drake and C.G. did not follow them.

"Aren't you two coming?" Jane Grady asked.

C.G. and Drake were gazing at each other with unmistakable love in their eyes.

"We'll be right there," Drake said. "I have a very important question to ask of C.G. But first, she and I have a confession to make," and they told their mothers about working together, and falling in love, which was why they had had no interest in meeting this "perfect" man and woman who'd been picked out for them.

The mothers were unbelieving, then amazed, then intrigued, then delighted at how the situation had turned out.

As they walked away from their happy children, they giggled softly and winked at each other, and Jane said to Katherine, "They're a match made in heaven, don't you agree?"

"Absolutely. Isn't it fortunate we got them together?"

With self-satisfied grins, they made their way to their seats in the sanctuary just as the orchestra music began.

Back in the fellowship hall, which was entirely empty now, Drake took C.G. in his arms, kissed her hungrily and asked,

"You will marry me, won't you Chrysanthemum Geraldine?"

Looking into his powerfully persuasive eyes, C.G. murmured, "Yes, Drake Forrest. And thank you."

"For what?"

"Helping me redeem my honor and my career. I love you."

"And I love you."

Drake took C.G. into his arms, and they stood together in the center of the room and listened to the swelling of the music as it magnificently portrayed the glory of God.

The miracle of Christmas became the miracle of their finding each other, and coming to love each other despite unforeseen obstacles.

Silently they pledged themselves to serve forever this Christ, born to set them free, and give them life everlasting.

A Letter To Our Readers

Dear Reader:

In order that we might better contribute to your reading enjoyment, we would appreciate your taking a few minutes to respond to the following questions. When completed, please return to the following:

Rebecca Germany, Editor
Heartsong Presents
P.O. Box 719
Uhrichsville, Ohio 44683

1. Did you enjoy reading *A Match Made in Heaven*?
   ☐ Very much. I would like to see more books
      by this author!
   ☐ Moderately
      I would have enjoyed it more if _____

   _____

2. Are you a member of *Heartsong Presents*? Yes   No
   If no, where did you purchase this book? _____

   _____

3. What influenced your decision to purchase this
   book? (Check those that apply.)

   ☐ Cover   ☐ Back cover copy

   ☐ Title   ☐ Friends

   ☐ Publicity   ☐ Other _____

4. On a scale from 1 (poor) to 10 (superior), please rate the following elements.

____Heroine   ____Plot

____Hero   ____Inspirational theme

____Setting   ____Secondary characters

5. What settings would you like to see covered in *Heartsong Presents* books?

_____

_____

6. What are some inspirational themes you would like to see treated in future books?_____

_____

_____

7. Would you be interested in reading other *Heartsong Presents* titles?   ❑ Yes   ❑ No

8. Please check your age range:
❑ Under 18   ❑ 18-24   ❑ 25-34
❑ 35-45   ❑ 46-55   ❑ Over 55

9. How many hours per week do you read? ————

Name _____

Occupation _____

Address _____

City _____ State _____ Zip _____

Sally Laity

___*Reflections of the Heart*—Raine Montrose wants to live life only for herself until she meets Alan Decker. Badly scarred from the fire that claimed his young wife, Dek is also at a crossroads in his life. Together Raine and Dek form a friendship based on mutual need. . .until the need becomes commitment. HP4 $2.95 (contemporary)

___*Dream Spinner*—Amid the rural poverty of northeastern Pennsylvania in 1892, Starlight Wells shares a ramshackle abode with her crippled father. Far removed from the derring-do of armor-clad heroes, her dreams are but a reprieve from an ever-worsening existence. And then one day he comes. Astride his silver charger, her knight wields a Bible not a sword. HP31 $2.95 (historical)

___*Better Than Friends*—Callie's move to a condo close to her fashion boutique is supposed to make life easier. What she doesn't realize is that her next-door neighbor is a man from her past she'd rather forget. Is it possible Lex Sheridan has changed from childhood terror to the perfect gentleman? HP81 $2.95 (contemporary)

....Hearts♥ng ....

HEARTSONG PRESENTS TITLES AVAILABLE NOW:

······· Presents ·········

Great Inspirational Romance at a Great Price!

Heartsong Presents books are inspirational romances in contemporary and historical settings, designed to give you an enjoyable, spirit-lifting reading experience. You can choose from 100 wonderfully written titles from some of today's best authors like Colleen L. Reece, Brenda Bancroft, Janelle Jamison, and many others.

When ordering quantities less than twelve, above titles are $2.95 each.

SEND TO: Heartsong Presents Reader's Service
P.O. Box 719, Uhrichsville, Ohio 44683

Please send me the items checked above. I am enclosing $_____
(please add $1.00 to cover postage per order. OH add 6.5% tax. PA and NJ add 6%.). Send check or money order, no cash or C.O.D.s please.
To place a credit card order, call 1-800-847-8270.

NAME _____

ADDRESS _____

CITY/STATE_____ ZIP _____

Heartsong Presents
Love Stories Are Rated G!

That's for godly, gratifying, and of course, great! If you love a thrilling love story, but don't appreciate the sordidness of popular paperback romances, **Heartsong Presents** is for you. In fact, **Heartsong Presents** is the *only inspirational romance book club*, the only one featuring love stories where Christian faith is the primary ingredient in a marriage relationship.

Sign up today to receive your first set of four, never before published Christian romances. Send no money now; you will receive a bill with the first shipment. You may cancel at any time without obligation, and if you aren't completely satisfied with any selection, you may return the books for an immediate refund!

Imagine. . .four new romances every month—two historical, two contemporary—with men and women like you who long to meet the one God has chosen as the love of their lives. . .all for the low price of $9.97 postpaid.

To join, simply complete the coupon below and mail to the address provided. **Heartsong Presents** romances are rated G for another reason: They'll arrive *Godspeed!*